# *Stay Gone*

Stay Gone
A Necessary End
Don't Try To Find Me

Coming Soon:
This Is Not Over

**By Holly Brown**

*Stay Gone*
*A Necessary End*
*Don't Try To Find Me*

**Coming Soon:**
*This Is Not Over*

# *Stay Gone*

## HOLLY BROWN

*WILLIAM MORROW IMPULSE*
*An Imprint of HarperCollinsPublishers*

This is a work of fiction. Names, characters, places, and incidents are products of the author's imagination or are used fictitiously and are not to be construed as real. Any resemblance to actual events, locales, organizations, or persons, living or dead, is entirely coincidental.

An excerpt from *This Is Not Over* copyright © 2017 by Holly Brown.

STAY GONE. Copyright © 2016 by Holly Brown. All rights reserved under International and Pan-American Copyright Conventions. By payment of the required fees, you have been granted the nonexclusive, nontransferable right to access and read the text of this e-book on-screen. No part of this text may be reproduced, transmitted, downloaded, decompiled, reverse-engineered, or stored in or introduced into any information storage and retrieval system, in any form or by any means, whether electronic or mechanical, now known or hereafter invented, without the express written permission of HarperCollins Publishers.

EPub Edition NOVEMBER 2016 ISBN: 9780062655127
Print Edition ISBN: 9780062655141

10 9 8 7 6 5 4 3 2 1

## Rae

### Right Now

MY MOTHER IS dead.

The worsening of her illness was inexorable, and this ending inevitable. Hospice workers have been coming to the house for weeks—palliative measures only, the relief of suffering without treatment, comfort without cure. They were very clear on this point. There should have been no room for denial.

But somehow, when it's your mother, you deny until the end.

It's not like a dance recital, and you can practice, practice, practice. There is no preparation, not really. I've never lived in a world without her. Marlene Joy Kalatchik. Mom. Mommy.

No one else has ever leveled me with a look like she could; no one else could affirm or destroy like my mother. She was the repository for all my insecurities. She fed them, unknowingly. I like to think unknowingly. Simon says otherwise, but he first met her a year ago, and given the cancer, she wasn't herself. Not exactly.

My mother is dead.

I say it out loud, experimentally, full of wonder as much as pain. Impossible. I whisper it. I touch my tongue to it, like it's a loose tooth.

Simon is beside me, and he's got his arm around me, he's murmuring something, but I can't seem to hear it. I can't feel him. There's nothing but her, nothing but absence and loss and something else, just out of sight, just beyond my reach.

Natural causes. I think that's what the coroner will say, even if it was by her own hand. A hand that was coerced by someone else, or a hand that's an extension of hers, because isn't that what family is? An extension. A proxy. A way to go on.

Thomas is staring down at her, too, his expression inscrutable. No, it's not her. Already, it's her body.

He shouldn't be here. Why didn't he just stay gone?

I wish I'd said no, I won't find him, let the past be the past, it's just us now, Mom, and that's enough. I should have tried harder to convince her that I'm enough, though that had already been a lifelong project, a study in futility and false hope. I've been flexing my denial muscle for a long time. And yet . . .

I think I see Thomas and Simon exchange some sort of look. I've seen that look before. There's mischief in it. No, mirth. No, it's the satisfaction of collusion. Like they're in it together.

No. Simon's here for me, and Thomas is here for himself, just like always. Simon's mine.

And if I'm wrong about that? Then what do I have?

My mother is dead.

My mother's body is dead. Her spirit? Does that continue?

It must. Because suddenly, I feel it here. I feel her, like radiant heat whooshing up from the floorboards, filling the room. She's always been larger than life, in my eyes. Illness couldn't shrink her. Maybe death can't, either.

We were closer in those last days. She told me something I'd waited my whole life to hear, and now she has a message for me. There are things I've never known, and I need to. I've always sensed them, the secrets, like movement in my peripheral vision. I could never turn my head quickly enough.

But she wants me to know now. It's time.

I lean in close, and listen.

## Rae

### Ten Weeks Earlier

"YOU'RE NOT DYING," I said firmly.

My mother raised a skeptical eyebrow. "Are you in my body, Rae?"

"You're not a doctor, Mom."

She shook her head like I'd never get it. I was intimately familiar with that gesture, having been infuriated by it all my life. But I didn't allow myself those kinds of negative reactions anymore. My mother's illness had been my wake-up call. She wasn't going to die; this was all just a reminder that I was lucky to have a mother at all. Sure, she's feisty and opinionated. She's a force. Not always a force for good, but you can't have everything.

"You're only a stage III," I said.

"Stage III*B*." She emphasized the B and some spit landed on my arm. She was on the slate gray fainting couch, and I squatted beside her. My knees were starting to hurt. I wasn't so young anymore myself. Twenty-eight as of a couple of months ago, and getting married. This was supposed to be a great time for me. This will be a great time. My mother will dance at my wedding, her pessimism aside. She's always been a pessimist. Cancer doesn't change a person's essential self; that's what the oncology social worker told me, like a warning.

My father's cancer was stage IV when it was discovered. I was nine years old, and he was gone within six months. I'm sure that experience has only heightened Mom's natural tendency to look on the dim side. I tried to tell her that she's a whole integer ahead of my father, and today's treatment options are far more advanced. Put those together, and it would equal a long life ahead of her.

"You'll dance at my wedding," I said, and she let out a humph, the companion piece to the you'll-never-get-it head shake.

At fifty-nine, and despite the cancer, she was still pretty. Not handsome or attractive or any of the other adjectives usually applied to women of a certain age—no, she's pretty. Her auburn hair had thinned from the chemo but you had to know her well to notice; it was improbably thick before, with the perfect hint of wave. She's petite with delicate features, which made her personality seem even more formidable through contrast. I've always felt oafish, coarse, beside her, at five-foot-eight, though people have said I'm attractive, too—my hair long and fine, darker than hers, and my eyes hazel where hers are sea-glass green.

She'd have no trouble finding a date for the wedding. Since Dad died, she'd often had someone to dance with, for a little while. They never stayed long, and that seemed to be her preference. I had the impression every ending was either mutual, or her choice, but she probably wouldn't let on if it was any other way. Vulnerability equals weakness, that was the algorithm she'd lived by, and she'd die by it, too.

But not now. In many, many years.

It was strange, in a way, that she found my father so irreplaceable. Their marriage had seemed neither happy nor unhappy, more of a functional unit, in the traditional mold: He worked late every night to provide, she made a home. I don't have much insight into the inner workings of their relationship, since she never talks about him and I was only nine when he died. My perspective is limited by the narcissism of childhood.

In my recollections, my father was mild-mannered, and gentle with my brother Thomas and me. He pretty much always missed dinner but when he got home, he liked to read to us, his arms draped around each of our shoulders as one of us got the coveted job of turning the pages. He didn't like roughhousing, jumping on the furniture, or even loud voices. His own was quiet, and that's how he liked our home.

It's a surprisingly modest home, given the fortune that he amassed: two thousand square feet, a four-bedroom, in a suburban neighborhood close to San Francisco and Silicon Valley that wound up being yet another of his brilliant investments, now worth a few million itself. Apparently, he was a clandestine business genius, or perhaps he wasn't hiding at all; maybe he just liked achievement for its own sake and not because he wanted it on display.

There were answers I'd never possess when it came to my father, given Mom's silence on the subject. But I knew she must have truly loved him, because why else would it be so painful to invoke his name? Why else would she still be in this same house when she had the means to live anywhere? Sure, she'd redecorated the place five times over; she'd knocked out walls and redone the kitchen and bathrooms; her bedroom had been merged with my father's old home office (she now had a master suite befitting royalty); she'd filled the new custom-made cabinetry with expensive vases and statues and collectibles from her extensive travels, and the walls were covered with original art, so that her wealth was now fully, irrefutably visible; but she had never left.

When I looked around as an adult, I couldn't picture Daddy, Thomas, and me huddled up on the couch; the setting never triggered any forgotten moments. My memories have remained as sparse and wispy as my father's hair. He died young but he looked old. Or maybe all parents look old to children. You're always looking up, and they become dusty superheroes.

Thomas was okay while my father was alive. Dad's calm energy served as an anchor. After, my brother was unmoored.

Oh, and he smoked constantly. My dad, not Thomas. Cigarettes were pretty much the only thing Thomas wouldn't smoke. My father smoked so much that he not only gave himself cancer; he managed to give it to my mother, too, all these years later, when she's never smoked herself. Man, did that piss her off. She was so full of vitriol that she was banned, kindly, from two different support groups. The funny thing was, if it had been breast or bone or stomach, she still would have found a reason for fury. She was not built to commune with strangers, or to simply take her lumps. She's made to roar. That anger would carry her through to infinity, I was sure of it.

"I'm going to die," she said now, almost triumphantly, like it's a chip to be cashed in.

I tried to ignore the feeling in my chest, the one that foretold of a brewing storm. "We see Dr. Parma next week. He'll tell us how the chemo is working."

"It's not working. Trust me. A mother knows." It was one of her favorite aphorisms, and it was most recently and frequently invoked where Simon was concerned. "I need to ask you to do something for me."

I stood up, shakily. My legs had fallen asleep. I wasn't sure they'd carry me safely out of the room, though I really, really wanted to go. I tried to pump the blood back into them, discreetly.

"I just remembered," I said. "I really need to go. I'll see you tomorrow, okay?"

"When?"

"After work. I'll bring dinner."

"I have sores in my mouth, don't forget."

Like she'd let me forget the list of chemo-related discomforts and indignities. I felt sympathy, I did, but it'd be so much easier if she could ever suffer in silence, or better yet, if she could count her blessings (she had far fewer symptoms than most people with her diagnosis, hadn't even had a cough), or if she understood that cancer happens to millions of people, or if she could see how hard this was on me, too. If she could just see me.

"I'll make you a soup," I told her. "Something creamy, and non-acidic."

"My time is short, I know that." Her voice stalled me, unusually quiet, the equivalent of fingers grasping my wrist. It was a vise.

"You don't know that." But I didn't sound nearly as convincing as she did. It's a gift she'd always had, the ability to sound so certain, and it had been a large part of her power over me. When she told me I was good, I believed her, absolutely. And when she told me the opposite . . .

"What I know is, I've always had a strong intuition, and right now, it's saying, quite distinctly, that the treatments won't work." I was about to protest again, but something in her face stopped me. My fearless mother was afraid. Of dying? That would be normal, but somehow, I didn't think so. What could be scarier than death? There's definitely no public speaking in her future.

"It's time," she said, "to find Thomas."

I felt myself sagging. Under the weight of her request, and the weight of my own stupidity. How could I not have seen this coming?

She'd always loved him most. His absence couldn't change that, if his presence hadn't.

"If he wanted to be in our lives, he would," I said.

"This isn't about what he wants. Find him for me. Please, Rae."

"The chemo's going to work, Mom. You don't need to do this."

She fixed me with a steely green gaze. "What's the point of staying alive if I don't have both my children in my life?"

Her initial treatment had been radiation, but the cancer had spread, so now she was on to chemo. Only two treatments in, she'd handled them like I would have expected: she wasn't bed-ridden, only temporarily couch-ridden. She was going to live. Which meant that Thomas could be back in my life, for years.

"He's the one who decided to leave," I said. But I could see it was falling on deaf ears. She'd never listened to me like she listened to him. And I was the one who actually made sense, the one who went to college, and never to jail. I had a split-second's inspiration. "By contacting him, you'd be going against his wishes. Think how angry he'd be."

"It's a chance we have to take."

We. As in, her and me. As if I had any say in this at all.

She should go find him herself. A few mouth sores and the occasional nausea and fatigue aside, she didn't seem that sick. Plus she had plenty of money to pay someone to do it. It didn't need to be me.

Why did she want it to be me?

She'd always nursed a fantasy that someday, Thomas and I would be like other siblings. Maybe that was it. She thought that if I showed up on his doorstep, there would be some bittersweet reconciliation. The past would be erased.

"He doesn't want us," I said.

"You can't know that for sure, any more than I can know that I'm truly dying. They're just beliefs, Rae. They're conjecture. But I believe this is my dying wish, and you can't deny me. You wouldn't."

She's right, I wouldn't.

But it wasn't because she's dying. It's because even (slightly) enfeebled by chemo, she had a dynamism—a refusal to be ignored, to be passed over, to go unseen—that I'd never possessed, and had always wanted. One of the things I'd never tell anyone, not even Simon, was that part of why I put up with her was because I had a fantasy of my own. It was that her charisma would transfer to me osmotically, that I would become her daughter in more than name only, the same as Thomas was so fully, so obviously, her son.

"Veal parmigiana!" Simon called to me.

I breathed in deeply. It was a sentimental choice, my father's favorite dish, and one that brought me back to simpler times. Simon's a gem. He knew I needed simpler right then, even without knowing about Thomas. Just being with my mother every day was complicated enough.

I followed the scent and took a seat at the center bar stool where I could watch Simon work in the galley kitchen. The appliances were all new and stainless steel;

the black marble and wood cabinetry seemed high quality. It's a nice condo, the one Simon already owned when we got together. I wouldn't have chosen a gated community in Richmond, a small Bay Area city that's otherwise crime-riddled, but the community itself had a surprisingly bucolic feel, and I loved the paths along the water. Most nights, Simon and I walked to our bench and watched the sunset. Not that night, though. I was too late for that.

Simon was sautéing the veal, and the smell was incredible. I'd say it smelled like home, but that's not entirely accurate. It smelled like the Italian restaurant our family went to on the rare nights my father didn't work late, the kind with red-checked tablecloths and a host who greeted us by name in an accent so heavy that it seemed a little put on, theatrical, but we loved it, and him. Before my father died, we were still a real family; it wasn't nearly as apparent that my mother loved Thomas more. Much more.

"How was she today?" Simon's back was to me, so I couldn't see his face. His tone was carefully neutral. He always said that he had nothing against my mother, except that she had something against him, but I knew, all too well, how much her disapproval could sting.

I sighed. Should I tell him now? I poured myself a glass of red wine from the bottle that he'd thoughtfully left open on the counter in front of me. I saw that he had a mostly-drunk glass near the sizzling pan. I was not yet properly buffered, though he might have been. I took a long swallow.

"She's convinced she's going to die," I said.

"Sure."

"You're sure she's going to die?"

"No, I meant, of course she's convinced she's going to die. She always thinks the worst, right? The truth is, no one knows when their number's going to be called. You could die tomorrow. I could die tomorrow."

This was not comforting to me.

He turned the veal with a pair of tongs. I watched his well-muscled back in his fitted T-shirt. He's handsome, even from behind, and he doesn't look like a Simon. But then, what electrician would? His father was an academic and an anglophile.

I quickly drained my wineglass and poured another. As he layered the veal in a pan with cheese and sauce, he told me about his day. He's so good at filling his time between jobs. Right then, he was working on making a new dining room table out of reclaimed wood, and it was housed in his buddy Jim's garage. Someday Simon hoped to have his own garage that he could turn into a workshop or even better, a separate detached structure behind the main house. He occasionally sent me links to properties to ask what I thought. What I thought was, *We're not in any position to afford those*, with how stratospheric the real estate market is right now. What I texted back was, Love it!

Simon wasn't exactly slurring, but there was a looseness to his speech that wasn't explained by the amount of wine missing from his glass. I had the sense that he and Jim had had a couple of beers before he drove home on his motorcycle, which didn't thrill me, but I wasn't about to say anything. I had to trust him. He's a good person, and we were getting married, and I didn't want to be his mother. So . . . enough said.

Once the pan was in the oven, he came and sat down on the stool beside me. He took my face in his hands and gave me a lingering kiss. Not a mere "Glad you're home" but an "I want to have you later" kiss. It might have even been an "I need to have you later" kiss. It stirred me, though I'd never been that sexual of a person. After almost a year together, I couldn't believe he still wanted me so much.

"Now what's really going on?" he asked, his hand moving to my thigh. He turned toward me fully, listening with his whole body.

I had wine and sex coursing through me; it would have been so easy to say nothing. Instead I blurted, "She wants me to find Thomas for her. It's her dying wish."

"Except she might not be dying, no more than I am, or you are."

"But she thinks she is."

"Or she told you that to get you to do what she wants."

As if she needed ammunition to get me to do her bidding. He always thought she was manipulating me, but the truth was, she didn't have to manipulate in order to get her way.

Simon didn't really understand my relationship with my mother. He thought my devotion was all about the golden handcuffs, the way she'd give sudden lavish gifts at just the right intervals to keep me hooked (not too often, but not too infrequent, either). The car I drove had been a surprise present, and while Simon pointed out that she could have afforded way more than a Toyota Camry, I was touched because she had picked the safest car in its class. She was looking out for me, and in a pinch, she'd always be there for me, in her way.

Golden handcuffs could not begin to explain my attachment to my mother. But then, how could Simon be expected to understand? It was incomprehensible, unless he'd spent time in a cult.

"Do you want to do this?" he asked. "Do you want to find Thomas?"

"Are you really asking me that?"

"So say no. Say, 'You're not dying, and your son's an asshole.'" He squeezed my leg. "I know, you would never say it like that. But you have the right to say no. Just find the words. You don't want that guy back in your life, or in your mother's life."

He didn't know the half of it. He thought Thomas was only an asshole. I'd never told him about when I was fourteen, what Thomas and my mother called "my accident." And I'd never told him about my jealousy of their relationship. Because what's less attractive than jealousy? When I saw Simon at a party laughing with another woman, for a half second, I'd think, *Obviously he wants her. This has been too good to be true.* But I had to will those thoughts away, and keep moving.

"I just want you to be honest with her, that's all," he said.

"She'll wear me down."

"Don't let her."

I shook my head. "It's her life. He's her son. We don't know what that's like. We won't know until we have kids of our own."

"Five."

I smiled at the joke, not because it was funny but because it's familiar. Because he wanted to make me smile, and I appreciated that, more than I could say.

"She is truly sick," I said. "If seeing her son again will lift her spirits, maybe it's the right thing to do. It's not like I have to see him. Whenever he's around, I won't be."

"Maybe it'll actually make life easier for you. You won't have to be over there every day after work. We can see some more sunsets." He continued caressing my thigh, moving upward. "We've got at least another half hour until dinner's ready."

I loved Simon's touch, but Thomas and my mother were anti-aphrodisiacs. I hesitated. I tried not to have sex when I didn't really want to, though I hated to disappoint Simon.

"Let me handle this for you," he said. "You know I'm a master of Google Fu. I've got the time right now."

It was true, he did have way more time than I did. He never got stressed out about being between jobs; he knew more work would come, and when it did, he'd be paid well. He earned three times my insurance agent salary while working fewer hours.

I'd really started to hate my job. It's basically customer service, and I seemed to get the most entitled rich folks ever. I got people who bought multimillion-dollar houses in Seacliff and then refused to hear me when I told them that they couldn't get a standard policy unless they did seismic retrofitting to brace against earthquakes, that instead they were looking at something out of Lloyd's of London that'd cost an extra five grand a year, minimum, unless they bit the bullet and did what they should have done anyway for safety reasons, seeing as this was the San Francisco Bay Area, site of the future Big One, and they wheedled and cajoled and insisted that the requirement shouldn't apply to them and when all I could say was, I'm sorry but yes, it does apply to even you, then they told me, basically, to fuck off, because how could they be expected to spend another $30K to keep their houses from sliding into the ocean in the not-so-unlikely event of an earthquake?, and I said again, I'm so sorry, you're absolutely right, until they calmed down and then I had the honor of pulling together the best possible policy for them.

Much as my own job sucked, I still wished Simon worked every day, like other people. It would feel more secure. Well, it would have made my mother feel more secure, and less vocally critical.

If she had her way, I'd be marrying someone else, someone who—as she put it—"works with his mind instead of just his hands." I'd told her, over and over, that being an electrician is more about the mind than the hands; it's problem-solving, plus physical dexterity. Simon was the whole package.

Ironically, I met Simon through my mother. He came out to do an estimate for replacing all the old knob-and-tube wiring in her house. She didn't end up going with him. He wasn't the most expensive or the cheapest, and my mother has never trusted the median. She actually chose the highest estimate, and Simon later guffawed when I told him who she'd picked. That was on our third date.

But back to that first meeting—both mine, and my mother's. She liked him. She told me he seemed trustworthy "and he's easy on the eyes, too." That was before she knew that Simon and I had stood outside, leaning against his truck, talking for a half hour. It was before she knew he'd put my number in his phone.

Then, once Simon and I were together, my mother's opinion of him underwent a mysterious revision. She distrusted his whole trade, and thought he was "just a little too smooth, a real operator." She found the few one-star Yelps of him and left them up on her laptop for me to see.

At first, I thought it was snobbery, pure and simple. My father had been a whiz in finance, his collar whiter than white, and that's what she wanted for me. But over time, I started to think it was something else, something far more painful: In my mother's eyes, I was the one who lowered Simon; paradoxically, he wasn't good enough for me because he was with me. No man who would choose me would be good enough for my mother's daughter.

"It's going to be okay," Simon whispered, his face close to mine. "Don't worry, I'm here now. I won't let Thomas hurt you."

I wanted to be reassured, but there was so much he didn't know. I hadn't told him much about Thomas except that Thomas was someone who should stay gone, a troubled teen who'd grown into a troubled adult. No, that wasn't accurate. Thomas never seemed that troubled. He troubled everyone else, and that was okay with him. He was the carrier of the virus, yet he himself was immune.

The day I found out that Thomas had vanished—he'd been staying at my mother's house and he just up and left without a word, no forwarding address, his phone disconnected, poof—was the best day of my life.

It might have been the worst day of my mother's (I'm not sure how it stacked up against my father's death), because she instantly saw it for the hostile finality it had since proven to be. The death of her firstborn, her favorite.

And then there was one. Only me. I thought, *Now things have to change. She'll have no choice.*

I didn't know what had happened between them. She never volunteered; I didn't ask. The less said about Thomas, the better, as far as I was concerned.

To my shock, Thomas actually left me a few messages, saying that just because he was through with Mom, that didn't have to be the end of our relationship. He said, "Actually, it could be the beginning."

Like I'd ever answer those and form some unholy alliance with the bad seed. Like I'd ever turn against my own mother. I didn't tell her about the messages because it would have been salt in her enormous, throbbing wound. Sure, I'd passed up the opportunity to hear the truth straight from the horse's mouth, but then, I've never trusted Thomas's idea of truth.

## Go West, Young Man

Thomas Kalatchik, the 31-year-old CEO of **Piping Hot**, lives in San Francisco, so why can't he do business there?

To say that Thomas Kalatchik is not your ordinary San Francisco entrepreneur is like saying that, well, **Piping Hot** is not your ordinary food delivery service. They're both colossal understatements.

He suggested we meet for a bite at a taqueria in the Mission district because he'd been craving the taco al pastor, and because, as he said, he "likes quick and cheap." What he doesn't like is being profiled, but he's going to have to get used to it, as **Piping Hot** is currently valued at $80 million after less than two years. However, what's captured the business community's attention isn't just Kalatchik's success (others have risen higher, and faster), but that he's notoriously circumspect—some would say secretive—about the specific structure and finances behind it. Let's just say there's no IPO anytime in the immediate future.

Then, of course, there's his "product" itself: scantily clad women who could grace any Hooters delivering meals from local restaurants, at highly inflated prices (a typical food delivery service like GrubHub charges less than half the fees). "You don't have to consider yourself a feminist," says one outspoken San Francisco critic, "to consider this sexist."

He's also under scrutiny for his business model: Similar to Uber, he doesn't have employees but rather, contractors. The women use their own vehicles to make the food deliveries, and he pays them no benefits.

Kalatchik makes no apologies on either count. He is soft-spoken and self-effacing, but direct. "I'd hire men if there was a demand," he says, "but the market doesn't seem to be there. Women don't want their pad Thai delivered by a hot dude in tight pants." He gives me a crooked smile. "Do you?"

I can't help smiling back. Kalatchik could be that hot guy, truth be told: tall, well-built, dark hair, and piercing hazel eyes. This is a fact that hasn't escaped the notice of both his fans and his detractors. Some who've objected to the objectification that seems inherent in his business feel that he's getting a free pass because of his looks and charm.

"I respect women," he says. "Ask any of my contractors. This model gives them the greatest flexibility. A lot of them are working moms, and they tell me that this is perfect. They can drop their kids off and then do the lunch rush. Or they can fit in a couple of nights a week. The tips, they tell me, are amazing." That crooked smile again. "I give them a generous cut of the service fees, too. The funny thing is, it's not my contractors who are complaining; it's people on the outside who want to pass judgment. I tell them we should sit down and talk, but they don't want to do that. They want to talk to the press instead, which—no offense—isn't my deal. It's not how I want to handle things. I'm a straight shooter. Ask anyone who works for me."

"There aren't actually many people working for you, are there?" I ask. "As in, employees. From what I could find out—and admittedly, that's not a lot, you've kept things opaque, shall we say— you don't seem to have a lot of infrastructure for a business with such high revenues."

"I'm hiring. You know anyone?" He grins. "Kidding. I like to keep the overhead low, and my inner circle small. I don't trust just anyone."

Kalatchik is undeniably private, and his backstory is not well known. He's clearly not eager to embellish on it during our meeting. What is known is that he grew up in the San Francisco Bay Area to upper middle class parents, that he went to the "College of Hard Knocks" as he puts it, and a few years ago, he got his big idea. He wasn't a fixture on the venture capital scene, didn't have any failed start-ups to his name, hadn't even worked for one. He's got little interest in Silicon Valley or, for that matter, technology. His right-hand man is a close-lipped tech genius named Ben Hwang; no one knows how they met but it is clear that Hwang has been instrumental in the success of **Piping**

**Hot**, which does all its business through its well-designed app.

"Ben's awesome," Kalatchik says. His enthusiasm is obvious, and a marked departure from his demeanor thus far, which has been quiet and unassuming. "He's got tech skills and finance skills. It's like a magic combination. Without him, we wouldn't have been nearly as successful as we moved west. We're killing it in Denver."

Geography is another thorny topic. Kalatchik has drawn criticism for **Piping Hot**'s path of expansion, which suggests an uncomfortable elitism, a playing into stereotypes. He started with several cities in the South (Charlotte and Atlanta) rather than in his own backyard of San Francisco. He says this was a pragmatic decision, and that anyone who says otherwise is indulging their own stereotypes. "There's nothing hillbilly about Charlotte, or Atlanta," he told me. "Or Raleigh, North Carolina. Have you been there? To the Research Triangle? There are huge brains there, the kind that could rival anyone in Silicon Valley. I know when I'm outclassed, man. But you know, the South isn't as rough on newcomers. They were willing to embrace what we were trying to do. And they don't have nearly as much red tape. I always meant to get to San Francisco eventually."

"And eventually is almost here?"

"Almost."

Speaking of which, he's almost done with his

taco al pastor, and he looks ready to hit the road. It's a little convenient, that he has to go just as I want to ask what he thinks about the reaction he's encountering in what should be his home turf, the Bay Area. There are online petitions, threatened protests, and negative press. The blogosphere has been anything but friendly. Some have said that resistance in such a progressive enclave (where not only women but men overwhelmingly identify as feminist) was inevitable, yet Kalatchik didn't mount any kind of proactive PR campaign, and now he's on the defensive. In business, that's often the kiss of death.

If the rollout in the Bay Area fails, undoubtedly Kalatchik will get much of the blame for having remained such a reclusive figure. Some say he's unwilling to get in the necessary face time, perhaps arrogantly assuming that the story would be "Local Boy Makes Good." I don't pick up any whiff of arrogance, but it's clear that Kalatchik plays by his own rules. When he's ready to end an interview, it's over.

So I never get to ask him about the lawsuits he's already settled (without admitting fault) by contractors who claimed they'd been sexually assaulted during delivery jobs. Or about the talk of unionizing, and the backlash against practices some say are exploitative, like the dress code (how low-cut is low? how tight is tight?).

As he gathers up his trash and mine, he tells me:

"This isn't just San Francisco. It's also America. And the amazing thing about America is that we all have choices, all the time. We can reinvent ourselves whenever we want. We can drive for Uber, or we can work for **Piping Hot**, or we can decide we don't want to do any of that, that there's other, better ways to live, ways that are more in line with who were are and how we think. If people don't like what I'm doing, then they shouldn't work for me. They shouldn't order food from my service. And you know what? I won't bother them. I don't run around trying to convert people. Live and let live. That's all I'm trying to do."

Holy shit.

This was Thomas? My ne'er-do-well brother had reinvented himself as the CEO of an eighty-million-dollar start-up? This is America, after all, not just San Francisco.

He obviously charmed the pants off that journalist. I wouldn't be surprised if it was quite literally, if he ended up proofreading the profile from her hotel room bed. Not that he was ever much for the written word, seeing as he barely made it out of high school. Oh, wait, he went to the College of Hard Knocks. I can't believe he stole one of Daddy's expressions.

Then it dawns on me: That's who Thomas was channeling. My father, a man who never raised his voice, who was sweet and self-deprecating and forthright. Thomas is none of those things, because people don't change that completely. Reinvention, my ass.

His right-hand man, Ben? He probably did all the work, and Thomas got the spoils. I thought of those kids who'd meet Thomas at the playground before school so Thomas could copy their homework.

I would have thought it a hundred times more likely that Thomas was dead in a ditch, a John Doe toe-tagged in a morgue somewhere, than the CEO of a successful company, even a misogynistic one.

No, no, he *respects* women! He just wants them to have the freedom to make their own hours, wants single moms to be able to pay their kids' way through college on the tips they get from delivering pad Thai. As if they just deliver pad Thai. Knowing Thomas, they're also getting paid for sex. At the very least, they must be doing lap dances or blow jobs or something. Maybe they're delivering drugs, too. It's one-stop shopping, knowing Thomas.

I didn't recognize the man in that profile, but I know Thomas.

He definitely had sex with that journalist. He's always been good at figuring out what women wanted and spoon-feeding it to them, so adept at getting what he wanted: sex, or money, or drugs, or a flattering profile in some online business magazine. My mother used to eat out of his hand, but not me. Never me. That's why he'd turned on me, and I was lucky to be alive.

A shiver went through me. I might not be so lucky this time.

"Hey, Rae."

I jumped three feet. It was only Donna, and not my

supervisor Antonio, but still. She could see my computer screen, and what was on it was obviously not work.

"Are you okay?" she asked, concerned. "You're white as a sheet."

"I'm okay." Then I saw the opening. "Actually, I'm not feeling well. I'm going to head home early." I started to shut down the computer. I thought of printing out the article but so much of it was burned in my memory. "Could you tell Antonio I had to go?" I didn't wait for her assent, just grabbed my purse from under my desk and raced for the elevator.

Once inside, I texted Simon: Need to talk to you NOW. Are you home?

No. But I can get there fast.

I didn't want to think about how he was about to drive on his motorcycle. I almost typed Take your time, but then didn't.

Practically the only advantage of my job was the short commute. I was home within ten minutes. Simon was home in fifteen, and I was in the living room where I'd alternated between standing and sitting for the previous five. I didn't know how to do this, how to confront him. I'd never had to before. Also, I was still reeling from what I'd found out about Thomas. That I'd found him at all, and so easily. Which meant Simon had lied when he told me there was nothing online about Thomas. What other explanation could there be?

Simon started by giving me a hug. He could see I

needed one, but I remained rigid in his arms. Another first in our relationship.

I couldn't—wouldn't—let Thomas screw this up for me. Simon was going to be my husband. So there had to be an explanation.

"I Googled Thomas," I said. Simon's arms dropped and he took a step back.

He looked down at the carpet, guilty as charged. "Did I do the wrong thing?"

"By lying to me?"

"By telling you what you wanted to hear. You didn't want him found."

My tongue was tied. I'd always been terrible at confrontation, just wishing things would go away, a crocodile slipping back beneath the swamp water.

Simon looked chastened. I thought of one of my mother's main objections to our relationship: that we'd moved too fast. "What kind of man asks you to marry him after six months?" she'd asked. "What do you know about him, really?" I knew what felt. This was a good man.

"I'm sorry I lied," he said. He just looked so sincere! I had to be right about him. "It was to protect you. I wanted you to be able to go to your mother and tell her, honestly, that you'd tried. You'd have a clean conscience."

"But . . ." There was something clearly wrong about his decision, and yet his lie was born of love.

"You haven't been sleeping. If just the thought of him is eating you up, then how bad would it be if you actually had him around again? I didn't want that for you. But I knew you wouldn't lie to your mother."

"You were making it so I wouldn't have to." That was, I had to admit, about the best explanation I could have hoped for. "And now I ruined it. I had to go and Google him myself." I sat down heavily on the couch. "Why did I do that?"

Because on some level, I hadn't trusted Simon's answer the previous day. I hadn't believed him when he told me that he couldn't find Thomas.

On a positive note, that meant that Simon wasn't a very good liar. Which was comforting, since I'd grown up with Thomas, the world's best liar. He was so good that I'd doubted my sanity all those years before, and tried to just put it all behind me and out of my mind. I'd literally had to go to a psych hospital, that's how persuasive he was. But he'd never truly convinced me, only our mother. My heart knew what it knew.

"I can't believe he didn't even change his name," I said. "He has a criminal record. This country is too forgiving. You just go on your merry way and start a company and no one cares that you were incarcerated?"

Simon sat down beside me. He looked relieved that we were a team again, talking about Thomas instead of what Simon had done. "You said he wasn't locked up for long. When I did a search on him, I didn't see any criminal records so maybe he got it expunged. And maybe he kept his name because he wanted your mom to find him someday. He wanted everyone to know he was a success."

What niggled at me—if you didn't count what Simon had done, and I was trying not to count that—was that my mother could have simply Googled Thomas herself.

Wasn't that the most obvious place to start, instead of asking me to head up the search when she knew that my feelings toward Thomas were ambivalent at best?

Mom's on her iPhone more than a teenager. She posted selfies on Instagram, giving a thumbs-up while the chemo IV was in her arm. She must have already known about Thomas. She wanted me to see it for myself, to know that she was always right to love him more than she loved me. I was an insurance agent, and he'd started an eighty-million-dollar company.

No, she's my mother. She wouldn't do that to me on purpose. She was probably too scared to Google him, afraid to find out that her only son was dead. She looked afraid when she brought him up, didn't she?

Thomas had gotten piss-poor grades but he had never shied away from taking risks, and that's what it took to strike it rich: fearlessness. Me, I'd been anxious my whole life. I worked hard in school just to make Bs, and I was neither great nor awful at anything. I always had the sense that Mom wanted me to be more, professionally, but never knew what that more was. When she made suggestions, it was like they'd been plucked out of the air, dictated by whatever successful person she had just happened across: "Be an interior designer!" "Be a mortgage broker!" "Be a computer programmer!"

It was painful, having no strong aptitudes and, frankly, no consuming interests. And no confidence, that was the clincher. Since being with Simon, though, I was convinced that my best was ahead of me: I'd make a good wife, and a good mother.

That was still true. So what if Thomas was a millionaire. Who cared? It had no bearing on my life. Thomas was irrelevant.

But how the hell did he do that—get an idea, launch a business, expand it across the country? It couldn't only be a matter of nerve. It had to be that other guy, Ben Hwang, the man behind the man, the tech nerd basking in Thomas's cool. Thomas was a lousy person, yet he was managing to come out on top. How could that not bother me, at least a little?

"So you have a choice," Simon said. "You contact him, or . . ." He left the possibilities dangling.

"Pretend I never found him?" He nods. "I can't just lie to her."

"You can refuse to do her dirty work. Tell her it's too hard for you, and she needs to do it herself. She's the one he's furious with. So hopefully, she'll contact him and he'll ignore her."

"It would make her so happy to have him back." It hurt me to say it, like an admission of my own inadequacy. "I want her to be happy."

"I hate to bring this up, Rae, but there's a practical side to this, too. I mean, how much is your mom worth?"

"Millions." It came out just above a whisper. I didn't know a precise figure but it was actually tens of millions. Mom had always taught me that it was gauche to discuss money. That's because she'd come from a lot of it, deposited in a trust that she'd never had to touch because of all my father's earnings and investments, plus a generous life insurance policy.

As a rule, I tried not to think about how much she was worth. I wasn't just waiting for her to die so I could cash in on all I'd been through over the years. I wasn't in a pair of golden handcuffs, like Simon thought, and when she died, I'd be sprung. Thinking about her money—fantasizing about it becoming mine—would be like betting against her. I wouldn't let myself go there.

"You're the one who's been taking care of her," Simon said. "You've always been the one she could count on, the one who never deserted her. And now he's going to just swoop in?"

Thomas would be the White Knight, and I would be cast aside. I wanted to tell Simon no, that wouldn't happen, my mother appreciates all I've done. But when it came to Thomas, all bets were off.

"He's probably not even in her will right now," Simon said.

I could only imagine Mom's reaction if she'd overheard this conversation. At a minimum, it would confirm for her that Simon had no class. People with class didn't talk about money. They certainly didn't talk about money and death in the same sentence. She'd stopped just short of calling him a gold digger before.

But she was wrong about Simon. He took a lot of pride in his work, and he was confident in his earning potential. He could take on more jobs whenever he wanted to, and he would, once we were ready to have kids. Most importantly, he was looking out for my interests more than anyone ever had.

"You saw the article," I said. "Thomas doesn't need her money. That means he probably won't even call back."

"People always need more money." I didn't say anything. "You've decided, haven't you? You're going to call." I thought I caught just the slightest trace of disapproval in Simon's face—I've always been acutely sensitive to that—but it disappeared so quickly that I probably imagined it. "I'm on your side, Rae. Whatever you decide is right."

EASY AS THOMAS was to find, he was (fortunately) much harder to reach. Maybe it was that way with all CEOs, I had no way of knowing.

There was no phone number for his company, no e-mail, and no physical address for a headquarters. The Web site was extremely bare bones, almost like an in-joke, as if Web sites were so prehistoric that he couldn't even be bothered. I had to send a message through the app. The Piping Hot logo was a branding iron with the words imprinted inside; I could practically smell the burning flesh of cattle. I felt sick.

This is for Thomas Kalatchik, I wrote. This is his sister Rae. He needs to get in touch with me ASAP. It's about our mother.

I hoped that whoever read it would think I was a quack, and discard it. Then I could tell my mother that I'd tried. I'd say that Thomas was like Fort Knox; I couldn't get to him. She'd know that her son was just that important, that he'd made it. That, in itself, was a gift.

Still, I dreaded telling her. The comparisons to my own life, my own success (or lack thereof), seemed inevitable. She'd have me by her side, but she'd want him. Just like always.

What had happened between them? They were so close in the months before he just up and left. Thomas was living in her house, they were spending all their time together, doing things like movie nights—movie nights!—and he'd cut off all his old friends, the ones she persisted in calling "bad influences," and she was convinced he wasn't using drugs anymore. He was learning to cook—to cook!—and the two of them were thick as thieves.

Then he disappeared, without a trace. Of course in the beginning, I asked what happened, but she just squeezed her lips together so tightly that the edges turned white. I could only assume there'd been some kind of a fight, or that he'd stolen from her. He had to have gone back to his old ways. It was clear that she was in deep mourning, so I progressed from thinking that she'd kicked him out to knowing that he'd chosen to leave.

Now, just under four years later, he had life by the balls. How did that even happen? With a toothy grin, a penchant for manipulation, and a disdain for hard work?

Several days passed and I stopped checking my phone anxiously. I went about my usual routine—taking my mother to her appointments, bringing her soup, hanging out with Simon—and I thought maybe it was all going to be okay.

Then I got a text:

Hi, Rae. Thomas here. What's up?

As if we'd just been in touch a few days before. It was classic Thomas.

Mom says she's dying.

No casual pose here. No niceties. I was discharging an obligation, and that was all.

She says it, or it's true?

As if she was the liar, and not him. Mom's honest, to a fault. Blunt. Where did he get off impugning her character?

She's got stage III lung cancer.

Shit. Was that it? Were we done here? Thanks for letting me know. It's not a good time right now.

Not a good time? She's dying, Thomas. You think it's a good time for her?

I appreciate you getting in touch. Take care.

And poof, just like that he was gone. Again.

MY MOTHER HAD been on the fainting couch more often this week. She seemed depleted, aged. I didn't know if it was from the treatment, or the stress of waiting to hear about Thomas.

I knelt in front of her. I didn't know how I kept ending up in such a penitent posture. It was probably because she never made any room for me on the couch, and the next closest piece of furniture was too far away for the intimacy of what I needed to tell her.

I rearranged the gray cashmere throw on top of her, staying close, stalling.

"Just say it," she told me, her voice hoarse. Her eyelids drooped, like she was tired just from the imagining. That's what she'd probably been doing ever since she made her request of me, imagining and suffering. I couldn't prolong that anymore.

"I've got good news and I've got bad news," I said, trying to smile. She used to say that to us when we were younger. Then there was "I've got bad news and I've got bad news." I couldn't recall a "good news/good news" delivery. I smoothed the cashmere. "Which do you want first?"

"The bad news," she said, like I knew she would.

"The bad news is, Thomas is insanely busy. He's under a ton of stress, traveling all the time. He's just got nothing left in the tank, or else he'd definitely want to be here." Thomas never said any of that, but it's probably true, all except the very last part. He most definitely didn't want to be here. "The good news is, all that stress is because he's a big deal. A total VIP. He's the CEO of his own startup, and it's a huge success. We're talking almost a hundred million dollars." I studied her furtively, trying to see if she had already known that, but all I could see was her pain. Her disappointment. The utter devastation of learning your firstborn, your preferred child, can't make time in his busy schedule to see you before you die.

"You told him everything?" she said.

"I told him it's stage III cancer."

"Did you tell him the B?" I nodded, a white lie. "He knows we're running out of time?"

"He knows you think so." She clearly didn't like that, so I added, "He knows it's advanced. I told him he should be here."

She grabbed my hand, looking deeply into my eyes. "Thank you," she said, and anyone else would have been crying, but not her. Not even now. I felt not just love for her, but pride. This woman was a warrior. Cancer wouldn't get the best of her. No way. "With your accident, after everything you've been through, you're still here with me. That means so much, Rae."

I could feel that her gratitude was genuine, and I wanted us to have a moment. I wanted to be suffused with love. But I'd gone ice-cold. After everything, she still called it an accident. That meant she was still siding with Thomas.

"If the police had been able to find that boy, everything would be different now," she said. Her eyes were closed, and she seemed to be drifting off, half asleep already.

"What boy?"

"The one outside your window," she answered, as if irritated by the question. "The one I caught watching you."

"Like a peeping Tom?" She nodded. "You never told me about this."

"I told the police. I could have sworn I..." Her eyelids fluttered. "I must have been sparing you. You had enough on your mind. You were always so delicate. I didn't want to scare you, but I did tell you to lock your bedroom window, don't you remember that?"

I did remember that. It hadn't even occurred to me to ask why.

"He was on a ladder, peeking into your room. You were asleep. I took care of it."

"When was this?"

"Not long before the accident. I always thought they might be related, but the police didn't take me seriously. So I stopped taking it seriously, too."

How could I never have heard about this before? When my mother was trying to convince me of Thomas's innocence, surely she would have mentioned this boy. She must have been hallucinating him now because of the cancer, and the stress. Because even now, she wanted desperately to believe in Thomas.

"I'm so grateful for you," she murmured.

She started stroking my hand, and I knew what she was trying to say. She was saying I was a good girl, and she was glad to have me, and I took a deep purging breath before I soaked it up, marinated in it, did the backstroke through her approbation.

I closed my watery eyes, wishing this ephemeral moment would last and last, but knowing, every second, that it wouldn't.

I FELT A little on edge, thinking that Thomas might have a change of heart, would realize he did want to see his mother before she died, would want to wreak just a last bit of havoc in our lives, but with each day, that fear faded. Mom was being kind to me, and my denial was holding up quite well, thank you: She would live, and she'd appreciate the child she did have, the one who'd been by her side all along, who'd given her—well, if not joy, exactly, then very little trouble. Thomas could bring about the highest highs and the lowest lows for her, but what he couldn't provide was constancy. When you're fighting cancer, you don't need drama; you need a consistent presence. That was me.

We met with Dr. Parma on a Wednesday. As usual, a half-hour wait in his exam room felt like two hours. He came in and washed his hands, like always, though he wasn't actually going to touch Mom. He was just there to deliver news. Bad news, as it turned out, and he didn't have any good to leaven it, either.

The cancer was growing right through the chemo, spreading. There were other chemo regimens to try, but the chances of success were low. Dr. Parma was no sweet talker. He was a pessimist, like my mother, and that might have been what drew her to him. Or maybe he just put on his pessimist hat to please her, in some perverse way. It was like how people grow to look like their dogs. Not that Dr. Parma actually looked like Mom. He was as wrinkled and homely as she was preserved and pretty.

"So what should we try next?" I asked him. Even if a chemo regimen had a five percent chance of success, that meant five out of every hundred people would benefit. My mother would be one of those: a defier of odds.

"Nothing," my mother said. "I'm done." It was in that same quiet, un-Marlene voice, the one she'd used when she told me we needed to find Thomas, the one so absolute that it stopped me in my tracks. There were no choices; this was what had to be done. Or, in this case, not done. Left untried.

I looked at Dr. Parma, begging him to intercede. He could certainly make a better case for continued chemo than I could.

But he was nodding, like he respected her decision.

"If she stops chemo," I said to him, "then she'll die soon. Won't she?" It was his job to keep her alive, not to stand by and let her die.

"If she stops chemo, she can die well. On her own terms. We can set up hospice, so that she'll be comfortable at home."

"I don't like chemo," my mother said.

"Well, obviously," I rejoined. "No one likes chemo. But do you like living?"

The room went silent, and I reached the conclusion that I had previously missed: Without Thomas, she didn't like living. It wasn't worth the fight if all she had was me.

It wasn't only me that was overshadowed by Thomas, though. She had friends, and male company, whenever she wanted it. She'd volunteered for years. She was in book clubs. She traveled. She did watercolor painting. She enjoyed fine food and the de Young Museum and the

Japanese Tea Garden in Golden Gate Park and watching independent films and Oscar movies. She'd elevated shopping to an art form. She had a life that she documented on Facebook and Instagram.

Yet it all came down to Thomas. He'd rejected her years ago, and she built herself back up, slowly, painstakingly, but this final rejection was clearly too much. To be told, essentially, that Thomas didn't care whether she lived or died had sapped her will to go on. What I'd taken for kindness over the past week was actually resignation. If he didn't care, she didn't, either.

The mother I'd always thought was indefatigable, indomitable, was giving up.

I installed her on a bench outside the cancer center while I went to get the car from the lot. It was a beautiful day, and she turned her face up toward the sun, like a daisy. Who was this woman?

I did what I only do in an absolute emergency. I stood just out of her eyeshot, around the building, in the designated area, and I pulled a cigarette from my pack. I lit up, inhaling deeply, desperately. This was the one secret I'd always kept from her. She'd be furious if she knew; I could just imagine her screaming, "Do you want to give yourself cancer? Well, do you?," while I shook my head like some sort of spastic mute. I was never able to form words in the face of her anger, and worse, her disappointment (the two were often conjoined; it was like being eviscerated by Siamese twins).

I couldn't hold out until after I dropped her off. I'd

just have to roll the windows down and chew gum and hope the chemo had affected her sense of smell.

As I puffed away, I could hear Simon saying that if she's ready to go, I need to let her, it's her decision. I remembered the time he'd asked with such obvious love, "Do you think you'd actually be happier if she weren't around? That you'd feel better about yourself?" Then I heard him pointing out that Thomas probably isn't in her will right now.

I ground the cigarette out under my boot, pushing all those thoughts away. The fumes had fortified me for what I needed to do. I had no choice, really.

Because this wasn't about money; it's about her life. If she died, that would be it. I'd have no more chances to change her mind about me. I'd be out of time for her to finally believe me, and to see the truth about Thomas. The most influential person in my life, the one I'd always measured myself by, would be gone, before I'd proven to her that I was good enough. Was Simon right, did I need a new yardstick? Of course. But you don't get to choose your parents.

Then there's the simple fact that I love her. She's my mother, after all.

Please, Thomas, I texted. We need you. She's going to let herself die without you.

The reply came back instantly, like it was what he'd been waiting for all along, for me to cry uncle:

I'll be there tomorrow.

Mom called to say she'd been throwing up all morning. I knew that it was from nerves, not chemo, but I told Antonio that it was the latter when I called out of work. Antonio's wife had died of a rare and unpronounceable disease so he was passionate about FMLA; I had all the leave I needed, even at the last minute.

That day, I would have much preferred to be working with underwriters—or even dealing with the most spoiled clients—rather than in my mother's bedroom, helping her select an outfit for my brother's homecoming. By the time I arrived, her nausea and vomiting had subsided, replaced by a nervous giddiness. She was like a girl going on her first date, and I was the one about to throw up.

"I'll just help you get ready," I told her, "and then I'll go."

"No, no," she said gaily. "I need you here!"

"You and Thomas always had a better time without me."

"No, no," she said again, but with less conviction. She held a pair of clip-on earrings up to her lobes as she sat at her vanity. (She didn't believe people should puncture their body parts, but she did believe in ornamentation.) I stood behind her, watching her in the mirror, the very same mirror of the very same Queen Anne vanity that she'd had when I was a little girl, back when I'd been transfixed by her preparatory rituals.

She'd since knocked down walls to double the size of her suite; she'd added an enormous balcony overlooking the backyard, currently planted in the style of French gardens; she'd changed the color scheme more times than I could count (right then, it was sage with dashes of lavender, similar to the gardens outside); and she'd replaced every other piece of furniture three times over, but the Queen Anne vanity had remained. And her rituals as she sat before it were just as hypnotic as they'd been when I was a child.

There was something in the deliberate, slow way she moved, like she believed absolutely that she deserved this time, that making herself beautiful was as important as what any other person on the planet was doing at that moment. She somehow managed to be unself-conscious and yet filled with such self-regard that it was breathtaking. She powdered like Marie Antoinette. She still sprayed on her perfume with an atomizer, but the scent had changed over the years—lightened, modernized. She switched out her fragrances during her yearly trips to Paris.

She held up the next clip-on contenders. "Do you like these?" she asked.

"They're a little much for daytime." As it left my mouth, I realized how spiteful it was. But I felt like she'd pinned me there, a bug on a windshield. I was being forced to witness their reunion.

She set the earrings down. "You're right," she said. "I don't want to look like I'm trying too hard." Then she turned to me and held out her hands. "Thank you again. I know this can't be easy for you."

Though my discomfort, my dread, had been written all over my face, I was still surprised—and grateful—that she noticed. Her hands around mine were so warm.

"He's come a long way," she said. "We all have."

Didn't she realize narcissistic sociopaths headed companies every day? Had she never heard of Donald Trump?

My stomach plummeted. She was never going to see the truth about Thomas, and her blindness would be the downfall of us all.

The doorbell rang. My mother dropped my hands and stood up, moving toward the door with a certain fragile grace. I saw her as Thomas would: the sweater dress loose on her frame from her cancer weight loss, the high-heeled boots that would have been more appropriate on a healthy woman fifteen years younger. It was all wrong, just like her miraculous recovery from that morning's emesis.

I followed her through the house, then hung back and watched them embrace in the foyer, watched her step back so she could look at Thomas, their clasped arms forming a bridge between them, and before they embraced again, I took him in: that same thick, wavy dark hair, the same hazel eyes (my hazel eyes), and the pale skin, untouched by sun, with no wrinkles or freckles. He was still tall and thin, in jeans and a T-shirt, though now it looked less like a uniform and more like an affectation. He could have afforded high fashion, the best designers, and the most skilled tailors. Instead, he looked identical to when he walked out of this very same door going on four years ago.

I didn't understand how they could be touching like this, as if nothing had ever happened. Thomas only showed up here because I practically begged him; if he hadn't shown up, I'd intimated that he'd be a murderer.

But then, he'd come close to murdering his sister once upon a time. Why was this so different?

Because they loved each other, my mother and Thomas, in a way that was sick and powerful and undeniable. As I watched them, it all came back in a painful rush: my mother's preference for Thomas, and his manipulation of that preference; how he alternately sweet-talked and treated her with disregard; the way she did her own sweet-talking with his school administrators and with the police, and on the few occasions that didn't work, she paid for the best attorneys so that he was never convicted as a juvenile, and then as an adult, he spent less than a year in jail. As she often reminded me, it was a nonviolent offense. He'd been talked into robbing that store by a bad influence.

His violent offenses were fights with people where no police were called and no charges pressed. They were with the kind of people who expected to get their jaws broken now and again; they'd probably done it to others in a big karmic circle jerk.

But I knew all too well that he was capable of true violence, true malevolence.

As he strode toward me, my stomach fell through to my shoes. I prayed that he wouldn't move to touch me, because I didn't want to submit and I didn't want to recoil. I couldn't show anger or weakness.

"Rae." He stopped a few feet in front of me, his grin as easy as the one that reporter had described. Then it faltered a little, and he said with a surprising gentleness, "How are you?"

"I'm fine."

"Could I give you a hug?"

I startled. He wanted to hug me? And he was *asking* first? There are askers and there are takers in the world, and Thomas had always been a taker.

It didn't compute. This was clearly a nice-guy act, and yet . . . since when had Thomas felt the need to act like a nice guy around me?

Seeing my hesitation, he said, almost shyly, "Forget it. Another time, maybe?"

"Maybe." I tried to smile, though my head was a Tilt-A-Whirl. The people pleaser in me was in revolt, telling me I shouldn't have rebuffed him, and I could see, in my peripheral vision, that my mother was disappointed, which only compounded the matter. But I just couldn't let myself buy what he was selling.

The New and Improved Thomas. The same cola in a new can.

Though he'd never bothered with a new can before, not with me anyway. Thomas was treating me like I had some kind of power.

I stood a little straighter. Maybe I did.

I realized we'd been standing in awkward silence, and I didn't even care. I was the New and Improved Rae, not scared of this man who'd once tried to kill me.

HE ONCE TRIED TO KILL ME.

My shoulders slumped.

"You're engaged," he said, in that same gentle tone, like I was a skittish puppy he was trying to coax into licking his fingers.

"Mom told you?" That was why they looked so chummy already. They'd been talking behind my back. Of course.

He gestured toward my hand. "It's the rock. Gives you away every time. Is he good to you, I hope?" And he did look like that, like he was hoping, like he wanted me to be happy. He'd never given a shit about my happiness before, and there was no reason to think he'd start now. There had to be some ulterior motive I hadn't yet detected. Whatever his plan was, I was part of it.

"Simon's the best," I said.

My mom actually had tears in her eyes, like this was some beautiful sibling reunion. My skin was crawling, and I wanted to get away from the both of them. Just like always.

The next week was excruciating. In one sense, I was grateful to Thomas. Without him, my mother would never have started the new chemo. But watching the two of them—their casual affection, their laughter, their in-jokes (how did they manage to still have in-jokes after all this time? or were they already developing new ones?)—was almost too much for me to bear. For a man who ran a business, who was in fact expanding a business, he sure had a lot of time to spend with his mother. Three, four days a week, he was in her house.

My mother was actually nicer and less demanding toward me, and while I should have appreciated that, it was conversely irritating. She was a changed woman; he was a changed man.

Yeah, right.

He'd always oozed what I thought of as smarm but others saw as charm, and he'd never aimed it in my direction before. But now he tried to engage me in conversation, wanted to know all about Simon and the wedding, and even about my job. "I'm sure you've got some crazy stories in the vault," he said. "With people and their houses, especially with what they pay for them in the Bay Area?" The more interesting he presumed I was, the less interesting I felt. I clammed up. I didn't want to give him what he wanted, not that I understood exactly what that was. There was also some performance anxiety, which really bothered me since I didn't want to care what he thought of me. I just wanted him to go back to San Francisco and leave my mother and me alone. I wanted to feel safe again.

Silence descended over the kitchen table, and I decided I'd be the one to fill it. "How did you start your business?" I asked.

"I just had an idea," he said, with what struck me as false modesty. No, it was deflection. Well, I could play Twenty Questions, too. See how he liked it.

"Where'd you get the idea?"

He shrugged. "Where does anyone get an idea? It just comes to you."

"And then how do you go from an idea to a business?"

"Rae," my mother interceded, like Thomas needed rescuing. From me?

"I'm just curious. I've never met someone who started a multimillion-dollar business. I just want to know how that happens, that's all. How you run it. What you do every day." Meaning, how do you have the time to be in Mom's house four days a week?

"You surround yourself with the right people," Thomas said. There was a glint in his eye, like he was actually finding me worthy for once. A worthy opponent?

"You mean Ben Hwang?" He stared at me. "I had to read up on my big brother."

Thomas's expression changed, like a window being shuttered. "Ben values his privacy." Then, more lighthearted, "I've gotta respect that, you know?"

No, I didn't know anything, and Thomas didn't want me to find out.

The biggest question was what he was doing there, because he'd never been around my mother without having something to gain. But what could it be? He didn't need her money. He'd never really sought her love; it had simply been handed to him in such overabundant supplies that it was easily cast aside, the way we tend to devalue that which is both exorbitant and unearned.

"You know what he actually said?" I railed to Simon as we split a bottle of wine in bed later that night. It was a new habit of mine. I needed booze to fall asleep, and cigarettes to get through the day. Earlier, I'd lit up in my mother's garden. It was like I wanted to get caught. "He evades all my questions, and then says that it's good to be back among family! And he looked at me when he said it. What bullshit!" Droplets of red splashed on the duvet cover, which was, fortunately, red plaid, a vestige from Simon's bachelor life.

"Hey, watch it," he said mildly. I wondered if he wasn't just talking about the wine splash but trying to let me know his patience for my nocturnal rants was wearing a little thin. I could certainly understand that. I was getting tired of myself.

I set down the wineglass on the nightstand and even though sex could not have been further from my mind, even though my rate of initiation was about ten percent, if that, I dipped under the covers. I knew that Simon loved me, that wasn't the question, but I also knew that people can withdraw their love at any time. Nothing is assured.

The next day, I overheard Thomas telling my mother about how much stress he was under. His office had a flaming Molotov cocktail thrown at it—ineptly, since it somehow bounced off, no damage done. He really did sound worried, but you could never take anything Thomas said at face value.

My mother was lavishly sympathetic but I was thinking, *What office?* I hadn't been able to find any headquarters listed anywhere online, and when I put Simon on the case, he hadn't, either. I'd be inclined to think that Thomas's business was just some sort of a hoax, but that article hadn't been. And there had been others like it. Piping Hot was real. So what was really going on here? I couldn't take it anymore, the not knowing. I couldn't take having Thomas in my life again.

That night, I didn't just rant; I broke down. I confided to Simon what I'd never told anyone before, because the shame was too great: that Thomas had tried to kill me, and that my mother knew it. That was the true shame of it. What kind of person was my mother to spring into action to defend Thomas while I was still in the ICU? What kind of person was I, of what dubious value? And what did it say about me, that I continued to chase her love like a dog chasing her tail?

"But it's different now," I told Simon, my face tearstained but resolved. "He's up to something, I can feel it, and I'm not letting him get away with it. I'm going to stop him, whatever I have to do, and she's going to be grateful to me for showing her what he really is. He's not going to waltz in here, take all the oxygen"—all her love, I meant, but it was too pathetic to verbalize—"and then waltz out with all her money." He didn't need that money; I did. He hadn't earned it; I had.

Not that it was about money, but that was one big way to show love, wasn't it? And love couldn't buy you a new house.

I wanted out of Richmond. I wanted a house with a workshop for Simon, and I wanted babies. Ideally, Mom would live a long, long time, but if not, if all chemo was doomed to failure, then I would need all the consolation I could get.

Simon reached for me. "You're right," he said. "It is different now. You've got me."

# THIS NOTEBOOK IS THE PROPERTY OF ALFRED KALATCHIK

*For use only by its intended recipient,
my beloved Marlene Kalatchik.
Burn fully to ash after reading.*

*This is not my final will and testament, it is not legally binding. It is simply an expression of my fullest love for you, and for the children, and of my deepest wishes.*

*You have been so good to me, Marlene. You've seen me at my weakest, and never turned away. You have borne more than any wife—any person—should have to. I fear I have also put undue stress on Thomas and Rae. They're good children. I have seen, have viscerally felt, their kindness. They will grow up to be loving, honest people. I have every faith you will raise them well, Marlene.*

*Please follow the instructions contained herein. Once it's all been burned to ash, you only need to remember two things:*

*I love you and the children most deeply.*
*It's all for the best.*

## *Thomas*

### Right Now

I CAN FEEL Rae's shock. It's so strong, it's got its own smell, like burning rubber. Denial stinks.

Me, I'm not shocked at all.

For one thing, the woman had stage IV cancer. It barreled through the chemo, right from stage III*B* (she was always stressing that B, like a badge of friggin' honor) to the last stop, a locomotive that was going to reach its destination no matter what. Those cells were unstoppable. You could almost admire cancer. It's a thing of beauty, that kind of determination.

Rae thought our mother was the thing that was unstoppable. It's like Rae didn't even know Mom was human. What do you say to a person who just doesn't get it, at all?

I've been trying, though. To talk to Rae. To get to know her. To feel her out. To see if she's ready to get it. She'd be better off. Does she even register the fact that

I wasn't always the best brother but I'm trying here and now? That when Mom is gone, we're what's left?

It wasn't right, what went on in that house while we were growing up—me being so close to my mother, being her confidant from way too far back, before I could even understand much of what she was really saying. You hear all kinds of shit you never should have heard, things you wish could be unsaid, rewound, could travel backward through the air in slow motion, Matrix-style, back into her mouth. It's unnatural, that kind of closeness. But I put up with it, for all different reasons. Sometimes because I liked it, being the chosen one; sometimes I liked her, how she's feisty and funny; sometimes I felt sorry for her; sometimes I needed her help and I was willing to be as phony as it took to get it; and sometimes I was a dick to her and she didn't even care, she still kept talking, like she couldn't control herself. That's what must have happened four years ago, a bout of verbal diarrhea, but that was it for me. She couldn't tell me something like that and expect me to keep sleeping under her roof, eating her food, listening to her nasty mouth. That was the end.

Well, it was supposed to have been the end. Then she had Rae do her dirty work and bring me back into the fold.

Rae doesn't get the most basic information about how my mother works. Mom thrives on Rae's insecurity. She thrills at Rae's need for her approval. Meanwhile, Mom's always wanted my approval. Male approval. It was this fucked-up triangle and Rae just kept playing into it, playing her role, giving Mom what she fed on, like a vampire with an inexhaustible supply of fresh blood. I played my role, too, but I made sure to get something out of it. Poor Rae, I'm not sure she ever got anything but heartache.

There are lots of secrets, but the one Rae needs to hear first is this:

A mother is just a woman who gave birth to you. You don't need her to like you; you don't even need her to love you, not when it comes with that high a price. You just need to live your own damn life and find what makes you happy. Because a mother's just another person.

She was. And now she's dead.

I'm okay with that. I'm going to be a good big brother and make sure Rae is, too.

## *Thomas*

### Six Weeks Ago

DESPITE MY MOTHER'S addiction to interior decorating, the house was a time warp.

When it came to Mom, Rae was still the same insecure little kid, trying to be pleasing, saying one thing while clearly thinking another, all nervous smiles and shifty eyes. There was something kind of heartbreaking about it, how transparent she was, and meanwhile, she couldn't see through anyone. That guy Simon was obviously bad news, and she thought he's her protector.

My mother was just as self-involved and judgmental as ever, even with cancer licking its chops, waiting to devour her brain and her bones. What does it take, for some people?

I'd grown a lot since I last saw the two of them. I wanted Rae to see that I'd changed, that I was capable of caring, but it was hard to prove that when she was so eager to run out of the room the second I entered it. She'd be relieved to know I didn't plan to be around long.

Mom was pretty weak physically, even though she kept doing herself up every time I came over: all cashmere and makeup and perfume. We were confined to the house practically all the time. Occasionally we tried to go for a quick meal, and that was only on an extremely good day. She just picked at her food anyway, which wasn't much different from how it had always been. She was always watching her weight. Rae thought she was just naturally skinny, which is what Mom wanted her to think. I was the one who saw the binges, who sometimes even smuggled in junk food late at night after a raid on a convenience store. So what if I often stole the food and pocketed her cash, or bought some weed while I was out. I needed to have some fun, too.

Ben called and I told Mom I needed to take this, it was business. We'd been in the sunroom, playing pinochle. She taught me when I was eight. What kid knows how to play pinochle? Hell, what thirty-one-year-old man knows how to play pinochle? Next we'd be playing shuffleboard.

"Hey, man," I said. I went to the living room, the furthest room on that floor of the house. Even that didn't feel far enough. So I went outside and shut the door behind me. There was no way she could walk all that way in her condition.

It was the same street I grew up on, but some of the houses had been razed and rebuilt as McMansions while others had been renovated and added onto. Every lawn was incredibly manicured and the driveways were full of Mercedes, BMWs, and Audis. Dad would have hated all the advertisements of wealth. He made serious bank but he was better than all these guys, because he never needed to show it. After he died, my mom started keeping up with the Joneses. Her house had to be worth a mint by now. It's not that far from Silicon Valley, though it's a bitch of a commute. But everyone who lives here does it. People do all kinds of stupid things to waste their lives.

"Is she any better?" Ben asked.

"No. She's more tired. I convinced her to try a new chemo, but it's got, like, no chance of working."

"Sometimes it's just their time to go. The universe works in mysterious ways."

Ben was the only one who knew the whole story, why I tried to leave my mother in the dust. "I never figured you'd get all existential on me."

"I'm just trying to say, it'll all turn out like it's meant to."

"Like God means for it to turn out?"

He could hear the smirk in my voice, he knew me that well. "Let's talk business." He didn't like it, me mocking his higher power.

"Do we have to?" I walked in a circle, lightly kicking the tire of my mother's Lexus SUV en route. Across the street, I saw the drapes twitch. No one walks in L.A., and no one walked in this Northern California enclave of wealth and privilege, either. You drive, or you stay in your house. I was attracting suspicion.

"We might have to call off the expansion."

"We'd lose a lot of money, doing that."

"But we don't have the cash flow right now to go forward."

"I'm working on it." All we needed was a little capital to tide us over, and then we were going to take off in the Bay Area, just like we'd taken off everywhere else. Well, almost everywhere else. Chicago wasn't exactly a success story, which was part of why we were in this predicament. We'd find our way out, though.

"We need it now."

"So convince some creditors. We'll be good for it soon."

"Sure, they'll take your word on that."

I chuckled at his exasperated sarcasm. By now, we were like brothers. We could squabble, but we were bound. "Use your imagination."

"You can't put all your eggs in one basket, Thomas. You're not willing to do anything else I've asked you to do. We've been over this. You need to do more press. You need to suck up to some investors."

"What we need is for the expansion to be a success, and it will. Just keep working on the rollout, okay? Maybe we can speed it up."

"Are you even listening?" Ben didn't usually raise his voice to me. "We can't speed it up. We probably need to do the opposite. Retreat. Regroup. Figure out how to get more customers in the markets we're already in. Chicago could use some of your attention."

"Retreat is not an option." I made sure there was an edge in my voice, so Ben would get that this was no longer up for discussion. He was my lieutenant, not the general. "You need to figure out how to make this happen."

"Normally, I can clean up your messes, but this time is different. I'm pulling all-nighters trying to come up with solutions, and you're . . ." Brothers or not, he knew better than to finish the sentence.

"You think I like the way I'm spending my days? This was your idea." When he didn't answer, I knew I'd overstepped. He could be sensitive, and he didn't like being taken for granted. Time for a little wooing. "Soon, I'll do all the glad-handing you want. I'll suck up to investors. I'll meet with that weaselly media consultant again, and I'll do press. But for now, just do what you can, okay? I believe in you, Ben. I'm nowhere without you, I get that. And I appreciate the all-nighters. I'm not sleeping so well myself these days, so I get that, too."

After a long minute, he said, "I'll talk to you soon."

"Thanks, man." I paused. "Are we good?"

He'd already hung up.

I couldn't retreat. I'd be humiliated. Once the eyes were on me, taking on something risky like bringing boobs to the Bay Area (so radical!), there was no way to back down. I couldn't fail, not this publicly. Not in full view of my mother, and Rae. I knew Ben would make sure that I didn't. He'd been creative before.

I just hated meeting with those guys, the money guys, the ones from their prestigious universities, their eyes appraising me. They thought I wasn't good enough to be in the room with them, they thought Piping Hot was for the proletariat, the people well beneath them, but there were a lot of those people, and they were willing to make money off them, and off me.

Ben was going to handle it, though, so I didn't need to spend my time worrying. He was a genius, like my dad. Sometimes I couldn't believe I'd gotten lucky enough to hook up with him.

It was kind of crazy, how it all happened. I'd left my mother's house and gone to San Francisco, visiting meetings in the neighborhoods where I most wanted to couch-surf. AA, NA—I was equal opportunity. Sure, I had a minor problem with drugs and alcohol but I had a bigger problem with homelessness right then, and the 12-steppers were remarkably generous with me, especially the ones in Nob Hill, North Beach, and the Castro. The richer the neighborhoods, the more trusting the people. I got to stay in some great places, and all I had to do was say, "My name is Thomas, and I'm an alcoholic..." Well, I said a little more than that, after the meetings, but that was how it started.

Ben was a frustrated Web developer at a tech company. He was brilliant in both computers and business but totally underappreciated in his job, and totally into meth. I liked him right away, like, *really* liked him, nothing fake about it. It turned out we grew up a town away from each other; he thought we might even have been at some of the same parties but we were both too fucked up to remember for sure.

I stayed with him for two weeks straight. He actually had a guest room. Even the people I thought of as rich back then (now I've seen a whole new class of rich) didn't have guest rooms.

Now I had a guest room. In Nob Hill.

No matter what, I would not sell my place. I loved it too much. From homeless to the penthouse in less than four years. That was my story, and I was sticking to it.

One night, Ben and I stayed up late talking, and we got hungry. We ordered a pizza, and the delivery girl who brought it was in a skintight T-shirt that she'd cut with scissors to show her cleavage. Ben gave her like an eighty-five percent tip, and in her wake, I said, "That girl was not just hot, she was piping hot." We started cracking up, and then I said, "Piping Hot. Like GrubHub, but you're guaranteed some ass like that." I hooked a thumb in the direction of the front door. Ben and I were up until morning, brainstorming. He worked in Silicon Valley, he knew people, and he could shepherd me through the process. He handled the money and the tech; I was the visionary.

I intuitively understood how to appeal to men's basest selves. Ben couldn't do that. He was a good guy, the son of a Korean immigrant and his blond California wife, which made for a very strange physical appearance. People were always saying things to Ben like, "Are you . . . Icelandic?"

I can spot a good guy at ten paces, and an asshole at twenty. Ben's a good guy, and Simon's the opposite. I knew it instantly, even though Rae only brought him around the one night. The rest of the time, she came alone, with these tureens of weird creamy soups. Cream of cucumber, okay, maybe. But cream of radish?

As I was hanging up with Ben, her Toyota Camry pulled up in front. It didn't fit in with the neighborhood, that was for sure. My Hummer was on the street, too.

No one ever had two cars on the street unless they were having a party; their driveways were ample. But Rae and I were each keeping the coast clear, not getting too close, able to make a hasty getaway.

That's about all we had in common, really. That and the way we look. Everyone has always been able to tell that we're brother and sister, and neither of us bears any resemblance to Mom.

"Hey," I said, as Rae approached tentatively, a backpack on her shoulder, a soup pot in her hands. I always had to fight the urge to shout "Boo!"

"Hey." She gave me this squint of a smile and paused, uncertain whether she needed to stay there and keep talking or could proceed inside the house. She's always been this way—a lurker, a skulker, on the periphery. No wonder my mother spent so much time with me. Her other child's basically a ghost.

But there had to be more to her than that. I just never took the time before to see it. I had a lot of ground to cover.

Was that a whiff of cigarette smoke coming off her? Mom would shit a brick. She'd shit a whole house.

"I've been meaning to talk to you," I said.

Fear laminated her face. "What about?"

"How you're doing with Mom being sick. It's got to be hard."

She shifted the pot around in an obvious way, trying to demonstrate just how heavy it was, already planning an exit strategy from this conversation.

"How are you?" I tried to keep my voice friendly and

my expression open. I really did want to know. I didn't know that I loved her, but I didn't hate her. Mostly, I felt sorry for her. She was never really the same after that time in the hospital when she was fourteen. She hadn't been outgoing before or anything, but that's when she decided to become invisible.

She was kind of nuts even before her accident happened. She barely knew how to smile. She didn't seem to have friends. I once caught her using a razor blade to cut up parts of her body that no one was supposed to see, like the inside of her arms and the uppermost part of her thighs. And the day before her accident, she actually threatened me. She told me she was going to "expose" me to Mom. I laughed at her. "Go ahead," I said. It was pretty apparent that I fucked everything that moved and snorted everything that didn't. And whatever she told Mom, I could just turn it around somehow. My mother loved to forgive me.

There was this online chat room I went to in those prehistoric days when Friendster and Myspace still reigned supreme, and I would spill my real secrets there. I talked about how I technically had a ton of friends but I knew they were really a bunch of losers and delinquents, and I wasn't actually close to anyone. I always had a girlfriend, and I'd never managed to love anyone. And I was in this weird role with my mom, like a stand-in for my father, and my sister was a freak who slashed herself. You've got to worry the most about the ones like her, who hold everything in, not the people like me.

So that day, I posted what Rae had said, her crazy

threat, and added something like, "See, she's the one who's going to turn out to be the fucking serial killer." I felt bad about that pretty quickly, after her accident, and I stopped going to the chat room at all. Chat rooms were on life support anyway; I think AOL pulled the plug within a year or two.

Speaking of the walking dead.... "I'm fine," Rae told me, stiff as rigor mortis.

"You take really good care of Mom." I meant it as a compliment. If I didn't know Rae better, I would have thought she was barely suppressing her fury. At that comment? It made no sense. The girl was wound way too tight. "I just wanted you to, you know, feel recognized. Or something."

"Thanks."

"Are you still planning the wedding, or . . . ?"

The fear returned to her face, like she thought I was going to crash the thing. I didn't expect to be invited. I was just making conversation, which was more than she ever did. No, that wasn't exactly true. There was that one day when she started asking questions about my business. I wasn't exactly keen to answer those, given Piping Hot's current challenges, but at least Rae had looked alive, for once.

Anyway, this was excruciating. No more small talk. "Mom is actually dying. You know that, right?"

She blanched. "She's on a different chemo."

"It's not working."

"We'll find out when we see Dr. Parma." Her chin

jutted up just a little, defiantly. I was glad to see that much spunk in her.

The thing about Rae was that she worked so hard to seem like a good girl. I think she really was one, before Dad died. Afterward, she wanted to contain everything that was weird or bad or ugly, when actually, those things would have made her more interesting. To me, anyway. To Mom, too, I'm pretty sure. Neither of us were into this defanged creature, padding around the house.

I acted out, but Rae acted in. A couple of times, I tried to tell Mom how fucked up Rae was, and about the cutting, but nothing came of it. I don't know if she just didn't believe me, or was refusing to believe it, or she just couldn't rouse herself to take any interest in Rae. Later, there was no denying it.

"I just don't want you to fall apart when it happens," I said. "You need to be ready for things, you know? She's not IIIB anymore, she's IV, and she's super-tired all the time—"

"I'm going in now," she said, and then she waited an extra second, like she was afraid I'd stop her, or like she was daring me to try. I couldn't quite read her, and that was a new twist. I kind of liked it—not being able to see through her every second, straight into her insecurities and her longings.

"I'll come with you," I told her, and I walked a half step behind her all the way to the entrance. Then we did this little dance where we were both reaching for the door and I made a mock-gracious "after you" gesture and she pushed it open without looking at me or laughing at the awkwardness. She was like an android or something. But sometimes I thought I had something to do with that, and I was part of what broke her, and this might have been my chance to try to fix her.

Which was why I hired the private investigator. That, and I've always wanted to hire one. It just seemed like such a funny thing to do, to open a case with a gumshoe or a private dick or whatever they called them in the Sam Spade books. Yeah, I do read. I love that noir shit.

It wasn't that funny, in reality. I looked up some Yelps and found this guy with an office in Richmond so I wouldn't have to pay him much in travel time. He was located in a run-down office park, and I just kept staring down at the carpet, which was really short and not very clean, the kind that's like scratchy Astroturf, and as he asked me all these questions I didn't know the answers to, I felt dirtier and dirtier. I was looking out for my sister, for once. It wasn't supposed to feel like this.

I wanted to back out. Let her make her mistakes. It's not like she was asking for my help; she couldn't end a conversation with me fast enough. I didn't want to be sitting in front of this greasy guy with the receding hairline and the sprouting gray chest hair, asking him to expose Simon. But I'd already taken up the PI's time, and I would have felt like too much of a douche if I just walked away. So I doubled down.

Barely a week later, I heard from the guy. He'd found out that Simon had two different child support claims pending, by two different women, and that one of the women had been hounding Simon. She said that she was going to tell Rae unless he finally started paying her, which sounded less like blackmail and more like just looking after yourself and your kid.

"What do you know about Simon?" I asked my mom over pinochle.

She waved her hand dismissively, her way of saying he wasn't even worth thinking about, let alone talking about. I felt a little pissed. She didn't care at all who her daughter married?

It wasn't like it was the first time I'd felt pissed at her and bluffed my way through it since coming back. I wouldn't have been there at all if I hadn't been sure it would be time-limited.

"I don't like him," I said.

"Reminds you too much of yourself?"

I glowered at her. "He's a dirtbag, and she's planning to marry him. Do you even hear yourself?"

She jabbed me playfully. "Stop taking life so seriously, Tom. It's way too short."

Another one of her not-so-veiled references to her mortality, meant to put me back in line. The annoying part was, it worked. I couldn't afford to get out of line with her, not now, not when I was so close. Not like in the old days, when I knew no bounds. She could feel the difference between then and now, and she was milking it. And letting me know that she knew that I knew.

I shut up and went back to my hand.

A few days later, we saw Dr. Parma. He looked like Gollum from *Lord of the Fucking Rings*. If it were me, I'd want a doctor who seemed like he had a few more good years in him, but thankfully, it ain't me.

Rae came straight from work, and she was in khakis and a button-down. She's a good-looking girl. Her hair's a little flyaway, but her body's on point. I didn't know why she did that, turned herself into wallpaper.

This time, I was sure of it: Rae had been smoking. It confirmed what I'd always thought, when I bothered to really think about her, which was that Rae keeps all sorts of stuff hidden, and who could blame her, with a mom like ours? And, I hated to admit it, with a brother like the one I used to be.

She didn't even look at me when she said hello. It was obvious she didn't want me in the room, didn't think I belonged there. I didn't entirely disagree with her, but Mom wouldn't have had it any other way and Rae wasn't the type to openly protest.

Mom was on the examining table, fully dressed (I wouldn't have been there otherwise), and Rae and me were sitting next to each other in the stiff-backed chairs. Dr. Parma was looking none too steady on his rolling stool.

"How are you feeling, Marlene?" he asked.

"Tired. I can't even beat this one at pinochle anymore." She motioned toward me. "Where are my manners?" Dr. Parma said with a sudden heartiness, coming at me so fast that I instinctively started to lift my fists in self-defense. Then I realized where I was, and who he was, and that he was reaching out to shake my hand. "You must be Thomas. I've heard so much about you!"

He pumped my hand, and when he was done, I said, "You've got good news and you've got bad news. Which do we want to hear first?" My mother smiled, but Rae gave me nothing.

"The good news," said Dr. Parma, "is that you've got your family all together, Marlene. Your beautiful kids."

If that was the good news, then I was right in what I'd said to Rae, and Mom was definitely on her way out. Rae looked crestfallen already. She bet against the house, but the house always wins. In our house, at least, cancer always wins.

"And the bad news?" I said.

"The cancer is growing, and spreading. It's a tough one, Marlene. Aggressive."

"Like you, Mom," Rae said. "You can beat this." But our mother was watching me, same as it had always been.

"You're right," my mother said to Dr. Parma. "I finally have some good news. Thomas is back in my life. What remains of it, that is." She sighed. "It's harder this time to make decisions. Last time, I was ready to stop treatment. To call it quits. But now, with Thomas . . ."

I could see Rae flush. Last time, when my mother only had Rae, she was ready to stop treatment and die. But now, she had a reason to live again. Shit, Mom. Do you have any compassion at all?

I didn't have any toward Rae for the longest time, either, but I grew up. It was clearly too late for my mother, in all senses.

Rae was glaring—not at Mom, but at me.

She's like one of those wives who finds out their husband is cheating and goes to beat up the other woman. It's just stupid. File for divorce, take half; he's the one who made the vow. Be furious with your own mother, Rae; she's the one who gave birth to you.

"Could you please tell us the treatment options?" Rae said to Dr. Parma, fighting to keep her voice level. She was definitely not the type to kill the messenger. The person she'd have liked to kill was me.

I should have asked Rae which she wanted first: the good news or the bad. Hey, the good news is, Mom has renewed will to live! The bad news is, it's because of the brother you despise.

That's when it became crystal clear, what I should have already realized. Rae truly hated me. There was no fixing what was broken between us. She wasn't going to let me anywhere near her.

The surprise was what a blow that was, so much so that I didn't even have to pretend to be sad for the rest of the time we were sitting there with Dr. Parma. I looked how I was supposed to, like I was already grieving.

Dr. Parma was outlining some options, like another chemo, or doing radiation in a bunch of different places, or searching for a clinical trial though he didn't think she'd qualify for any. "But we could try," he said. Then he brightened while he described hospice care: people coming to the house, angels of mercy really, who would make sure she was comfortable, that she didn't suffer unnecessarily, that she'd "die well."

Any idiot could see what he thought the right course was. More treatment stood an insanely low chance of working, and would make her suffer unnecessarily. What Mom needed was a good death.

I couldn't have agreed more.

But I stayed quiet. I had to handle this with some finesse.

Maybe some part of the sadness I felt was actually about Mom. Even if you hate your mother—and I did, I truly did, after what she told me almost four years ago, after all I realized afterward about her machinations and manipulations—that doesn't mean you never loved her.

I went back to the city right after the appointment and let Rae take Mom home. I could tell Rae wanted some alone time with her. The crazy thing was, Rae was competing with me and I wasn't even playing the game. At least, not that game. Rae could have Mom's love, all of it. It was wasted on me now.

I let myself into the penthouse and instantly my shoulders relaxed. Ah, home sweet home. But for how much longer?

I wouldn't sell it. I didn't care what Ben said about how urgently we needed the capital and that the real estate market was red-hot. Every time I walked in there, I could feel how far I'd come. It was like the biggest "atta boy" you could ever have, like my father wrapping his arms around me. It's Nob Hill, you know? Through the floor-to-ceiling windows, I had views of Twin Peaks, Telegraph Hill, and the Golden Gate Bridge. I ate Fruity Pebbles at a breakfast bar where I could look down on skyscrapers and straight out to the ocean. It's ultra-modern, all light woods and granite and marble and steel—"clean lines" if you liked it, and "antiseptic" if you didn't. Christina used to switch back and forth, depending on her mood. She's a woman of many moods. Tempestuous if you think that kind of thing is sexy, and a bitch if you don't. Ben fell squarely in the bitch camp. He wasn't entirely wrong but I still missed her. We broke up six, no, seven months ago, but sometimes when I walked through the door, I thought I could smell her perfume, and it was like a sucker punch.

The living room was all white because the interior designer insisted, said there was no other way to go in a space like this, and what did I know about a space like this? So I said yes and tried to keep my feet off the furniture. I had a roof terrace with seating for twenty, though I'd never had anywhere close to that number of people over. I didn't entertain. I just brought women up there. It always sealed the deal.

Christina was the only woman I ever loved, and she claimed not to care about my money. Ben said it was a reverse Pygmalion story, and I had to ask him what the fuck that meant. He said I was her project. For a while, she had me dressing differently and talking differently, trying to pass for one of those rich investor types, the kind who was born into it. That's what Ben said, anyway. But he wasn't really objective. He called her a prissy little bitch; she called him a sycophant (I had to look that one up). I thought I would marry Christina, I really did.

It wasn't just how she looked, though that helped. It was that she could be so hard, and then a minute later, so soft. The way she could change, the way she could melt—it did something to me. Ben said she was my new addiction but the thing was, I never had an addiction. Twelve-step was just a means to an end. I owed NA everything, actually, because without it, I wouldn't have met Ben.

So when Christina made her big power play, when she said she'd had enough of Ben, that it was her or him, I had to choose him. Piping Hot couldn't exist without him, and I couldn't exist, in my present incarnation, without Piping Hot. Now it looked like I might lose it all anyway.

No, Ben wouldn't let that happen.

He was at my front door ten minutes after I got home. You'd think he was at a stakeout.

"I'm going to have to change my key code," I told him, only half joking. I didn't really like how he just let himself into my building, especially not then, when I really needed to be alone. I needed to decompress, and think. And maybe feel, too. I had just found out, for sure, that my mother was dying soon. I might have had a say in how soon.

Ben grabbed me and gave me a fierce hug. I must have looked worse than I thought. At first, I didn't feel comfortable hugging him back. But then he didn't let go, and I was clutching him back, and *crying*.

"I get it," Ben was saying. "I do." He was stroking my hair, and I imagined it was my father, right there with me, seeing me through all of this. That's what I was hanging on to.

I released first, and tried to laugh it off. I was too

ashamed to look at him. Not because I thought it was such a big deal to cry, but because he thought I was crying over my mother, and maybe I was, a little. I was also crying over Rae, and over Christina, and over my dad. I was crying because I was scared about the business, and about my home. Nothing felt permanent, or even real. Maybe it had always been a mirage.

Ben followed me to the living room. I sat on the loveseat, and he took the couch, leaning forward, his elbows on his knees. He was nervous.

"What's going on?" I asked him.

"I wanted to see you in person. I wanted to look into your eyes so you'd know I was really serious when we talk about the business. But you're not in any shape for that."

"I'm fine. I mean, I'm going to be fine. It was nothing I didn't know."

"So you saw the doctor?"

"It's official. The treatment's not working. It's just about whether she's going to have a good death or a bad one."

"What's good? And what's bad?"

"Bad would be if she keeps polluting her body with more chemo and dies anyway. Good is if she just accepts her fate and people from hospice make sure her morphine drip works."

He took a deep breath, like he was debating whether to say something.

"Say it," I commanded.

"Which one is faster, good or bad?"

"The chemo probably won't make her live longer, and

it might even make her weaker. But if by some miracle, it actually works..."

"...then we're fucked."

I met his eyes. "Are we?"

He nodded. "Could you just ask for a loan, point-blank?"

"She's not going to loan me ten million dollars." If she somehow agreed, there would be strings worse than any venture capitalist could pull. "Besides, if I ask, she'll think that's the only reason I came back, and then I'm definitely out of the will."

"Are you in the will now?"

"I'm working on it. It's not something I can just come out and say. But I'm logging the hours."

"Could you work faster? And then tell her to go for the good death, the fast one?"

Ben and I had danced around this topic before. Ingratiating my way back into her will had been his indirect suggestion, and then when Rae texted the second time, I'd decided it was a sign. But this was the kind of conversation that would send you straight to hell.

"I don't know that she'd go for hospice," I said. "I mean, morphine? This is the woman who doesn't like to take an aspirin."

"Who doesn't want a good death? It beats the alternative, right?"

"She doesn't believe in doing things the easy way."

"You've laid the groundwork. You've played, what, a hundred games of pinochle? You've laughed at her jokes.

You're her favorite child. Would she really leave it all to Rae over you?"

I didn't like the avarice I saw in his eyes. "She's smart."

"Is the cancer in her brain?"

"The scan said there were a few spots."

"All right then." I could tell he was pleased. I'd never wanted to kick him out of my house before. "You've got to take this to the next level. We don't have much time. This is our only play."

"What if I'm willing to suck up to investors right now?"

"That ship's sailed. Our books are looking worse by the day. That's why I've been sounding the alarm bells for so long. If I'm telling you there's nothing else, then there's nothing else."

"Not a single potential investor?" That seemed hard to believe, but I knew Ben wouldn't lie to me.

"Any investor's going to pore over our financials with a fine-tooth comb." He gave me a meaningful look. I knew there were some things he'd done along the way that weren't exactly kosher. It was part of why we'd kept the inner circle small. Ben hadn't always kept his hands scrupulously clean, and even if I didn't know the particulars, I was implicated, too. "Even if they don't look that carefully, they'll see we're struggling in Chicago. They'll know we're overextended. And they're going to know about the Bay Area opposition."

I hadn't felt the impact when all the opposition was online; it had seemed abstract, not quite real. But the Molotov cocktail had rattled me, so much so that I'd confided in Mom, of all people. They'd thrown it at this building, at my home, since it was the closest thing I had to a headquarters. A lot more work got done out of Ben's condo, but no one attacked him. I was the king. The figurehead. They'd known how to get to me where I lived.

I shook my head in frustration. "Why's it so hard just to get a credit extension? It's not even that much money. And it's short-term. Once we expand, we're going to have the cash flow."

"Don't you get it?" Ben leaned forward even more, until I thought he might fall off the couch. He was legit angry. "The expansion is on hold. We can't afford what we've already got. Haven't you been listening to what I've been telling you? For weeks? For months?"

Denial. It wasn't just for cancer anymore. "I'm hearing you now."

"I know she's your mom. I know this doesn't feel good. But think about what she told you. Think about what she did to your dad. This is just deserts, man."

No, it didn't feel good. It wasn't good. But my mother was my last hope. Maybe I could ask her point-blank like Ben said, see if she'd give me the money instead of an inheritance, or she could become an investor, while she was still alive ...

No. Even with spots in her brain, she'd have lawyers look everything over. She'd evaluate what kind of investment I really was. She'd know that I'd been asleep at the wheel. I'd entrusted too much to Ben, who was a genius, sure, but he was also a control freak. He'd hired contractors but he'd refused to expand our permanent team. He'd done some things that were, in his words, "quasi-legal" but said there was nothing to worry about. I hadn't asked enough questions; I didn't know the details of my own business. Christina had warned me about this, but I'd written it off that she was just jealous about how close Ben and I were.

And we were close. We were bound, for better or worse, more so than in any marriage.

This wasn't the time to turn against Ben. I couldn't afford to. Ignorance was no defense in the eyes of the law.

Besides, I knew that he had Piping Hot's best interests at heart, and mine, too. He loved me.

As soon as it was all taken care of, as soon as Piping Hot was back in black, I was going to turn over a new leaf. I'd be fully involved in the day-to-day operations. I'd have Ben walk me through everything, and if it was hard to understand, then I'd take classes. Accounting, or business, or something.

And when it came to my mother, I'd just need to act faster than I'd originally planned. I had to make sure I was in her will, getting the lion's share, and leaving Rae with almost nothing.

Poor Rae. She didn't deserve that.

I'd do her a solid, though. I'd make sure she knew the truth about Simon. Saving her from marrying that guy had to be worth something. Not millions, but something. Later on, I'd make sure she got her cut. I'd take care of her.

Did I like this ghoulish plan? Not at all. Did I have any other choice? Not one.

The next day, my mother was too tired for pinochle.

She was lying on what she insisted on calling the fainting couch, and I was rubbing her feet. She could barely keep her eyes open—whether from the cancer, or because she was depressed about yesterday's doctor's visit, I wasn't sure.

In her weakened state, was that the right time to go in for the kill?

Killing a dying woman . . . it hadn't come to that.

"Mom," I said, "you've been through a lot."

She nodded, her eyelids drooping.

"I don't just mean with the cancer. I mean with Dad's cancer, too. Being on your own all these years. And what I did to you. Disappearing like that." I wanted to choke on my own fake remorse. This had better be the best acting of my career, for the most discriminating audience. I realized her eyes were now fully open. She was watching me with an intensity that I wouldn't have thought a woman that sick could muster.

"I told you the truth," she said. "I trusted you, and you turned on me."

"I shouldn't have done that, Mom. I'm sorry. Thank you for welcoming me back like you did, and not making me explain myself. But I do owe you an explanation."

"I've always told you the truth."

In her own twisted way, yes, she had. "I know, Mom. I'm sorry."

"Are you?" She raised her eyebrows, studying me.

I refocused on massaging her feet. "I am. I wish we'd had more time together these past years."

"Why did you do that, Tommy? Why did you desert me?"

"Because I couldn't handle what you told me. Because I was weak, and cowardly. What you did—it was brave." My forehead was beading up. Could she see it? Would she mistake it for a sign of my contrition?

"I thought so, at the time. Now, I'm not as sure."

I knew what she wanted, and I gave it to her. She wanted to make me say it. "No, you did the right thing."

"What's the right thing now?"

"You mean with your treatment?"

She closed her eyes again, like she was satisfied with what she'd drawn out of me. She'd won. I was thoroughly humiliated, so debased that I was actually massaging her feet.

"Is there really such a thing as a good death?" she asked.

"There are better and there are worse. I don't know about good."

She opened one eye. "Will you be there with me, at the end?"

"Yeah, of course." I had to make sure she was really gone, right? That she wasn't going to rise up like Lazarus or some shit. "What do you want to do?"

"I want to have more time with my son. We missed the last four years."

That's right, Mom. Turn the knife.

"I needed to come to terms with things," I said. "When I heard that you were, you know, how you are, it gave me perspective." It was time to take my best shot. I trained my rifle scope on her, looking her dead in the eyes. "Do you forgive me, Mom? I've never loved any woman more than you. You know that." I didn't have to force tears in my eyes; they just materialized. When you're on, you're on.

Reciprocal tears formed in hers, and she reached out her hand. "Come here," she said, and I moved from her feet to her side, kneeling beside her. It was a position Rae seemed to favor. "I love you, Thomas. What kind of mother would I be if I didn't forgive?"

I knew better than to answer that. I dipped my head. "Thanks, Mom."

"I'll do the treatment if you want me to."

It was a trick, I could feel it. But Ben had prepped me for this moment. "I've been doing some reading. I think chemo is breaking you down, and I'm going to build you back up. I'll feed you macrobiotic food, and supplements. There are all these stories about spontaneous healing, people who stopped doing their regular treatment and that's when they got better."

She laughed. "You never cease to amaze me, Thomas! I never would have thought I'd hear this from you. Alternative medicine? Really?"

"The traditional stuff is just kicking your ass. Let me take care of you. Let me build you back up."

She was touched. More importantly, she was considering. "What about hospice?"

"We can still have hospice in here. They'll control your pain, and I'll do the rest."

She squeezed my hand. Tears ran down her face. "Thank you, Thomas." I laid my face against her stomach and she stroked my hair. I was home, and she could feel that.

I didn't know how much time passed but I jerked my head up when I heard the front door opening. Rae came through the foyer and into the living room, with Simon right behind her.

She looked worried, as usual, and Simon had this cocky look, like he was getting off on being her rock. It would be a pleasure to expose him.

But that would have to wait. I'd done enough for one day.

"Are you okay, Mom?" Rae asked, like I'd just mauled her. I stood up and took a seat on the other couch, embarrassed to have been caught in red-handed manipulation.

Rae took my place, on her knees in supplication. Simon remained standing, surveying. "Hi, Marlene," he said. He nodded in my direction. "Thomas."

"Hey," I said.

"Mom," Rae said, "what did he say to you?"

"We were talking about my treatment. I've made a decision. I'm going to stop traditional medicine, and Thomas is going to move in and take care of me. Macrobiotic diet, supplements, the whole nine yards." She beamed. I couldn't correct her about moving in; I would just have to do it. I wondered if she'd somehow managed to find out about the state of my business, because she seemed so sure of herself, of her advantage and her power.

I hated her. And Rae, acting like she needed to protect Mom. Then there was Simon, with that half smile on his face ... I suddenly hated them all.

"No!" Rae told Mom. "You can't do that!" I'd never heard that kind of rebuke from Rae before.

My mother reared back like a serpent. "Of course I can. This is my life. It's my decision."

"We can't trust him."

"Speak for yourself, Rae." My mother smiled over at me.

"She is," Simon said. "For once, she is speaking for herself."

Mom looked over at him with disdain. "This is a family matter, Simon."

"I'm her family," Simon said.

Rae gave him this look that was full of gratitude and pride. I'd have felt sorry for her, if I hadn't still hated them all.

"I'm okay," she told him. "It's Mom I'm worried about."

"You don't need to worry about me. I'm happy, Rae. I'm going to have my son back home with me. I feel stronger already."

Rae turned to me. "What are you really after, Thomas?"

"He's richer than I am," my mother said. "He doesn't need anything from me, he just wants to be here."

If she really believed that, she might think all the money should go to Rae. This could be a disaster. I'd be stuck living with her, mixing up probiotic shakes, only to have Rae walk away with the inheritance in the end.

What did the will say? Did she still keep it in the safe?

Maybe I could figure out the combination, if she was stupid enough to use one of our birthdays. Or her anniversary with Dad. Or the date she murdered him.

"I don't need anything from her," I confirmed. "I owe her for the years we missed."

"This isn't about money," Mom said, "for Thomas." She sent a pointed look in Simon's direction. I thought I saw him flush, just a little.

"You think this is about money for me?" Rae asked.

That girl couldn't buy a clue, even if she inherited all my mother's money.

"Not you," my mother said. "I'm talking about him." She indicated Simon and then addressed him: "Do you want to tell her or should I?"

"She knows everything," Simon answered, but there was the slightest warble in his voice. He knew he'd been caught. He thought he could get out of it, though, with Rae being Rae. "We don't keep secrets."

"So Rae knows about the children?"

I had to stifle an astonished laugh. I wasn't the only member of this family who loved noir, and I wasn't the only one who'd had Simon investigated.

Rae dropped my mother's hands and stepped away. She moved closer to Simon in a show of solidarity. "Yes," she said, "I know about the kids. They're not his. Those women are opportunists."

"I've been insisting on paternity tests and they don't want to do them. What does that tell you?" I had to admit, Simon was pretty good at looking innocent. "I never claimed to be perfect. But I'm perfect for Rae."

In that second, I realized: Simon marrying Rae was in my interest. My mother wouldn't want Rae to have all that money if she was marrying someone Mom didn't trust.

I started to smile.

"We need to give people the benefit of the doubt," I said. "Innocent until proven guilty, right? Love conquers all?"

My mother's lip curled but she said nothing.

"I'm getting hungry. Want to order Chinese?" I rubbed my hands together. Suddenly, I was famished, and eager to get to know my new almost-brother-in-law.

I told myself that I'd help Rae down the line. After she and Simon got divorced, and once Piping Hot was doing well, I'd hand her a few million, at least.

I didn't like any of this. I didn't like scheming to steal from my sister, or pushing her into the arms of some psycho, or rooting for—maybe even expediting—my mother's death. But I reminded myself that she'd done far worse by murdering her husband.

She called it a mercy killing. She told me it was Dad's wish to die with dignity. But I wasn't a little kid when he died; I was twelve. I had my own memories of that time, and I knew that my father wasn't ready to go. He would have done every treatment on offer so that he could spend one more day with Rae and me. If I'd grown up with him, I would be someone different right now, I knew I would. But I only had his love for twelve years, because of her.

Dad wasn't ready to go. She was ready for him to go.

She couldn't stand being a nursemaid, having to care for someone else, not being the center of attention.

I couldn't believe I'd been so stupid, that it had never even occurred to me. My father was a stage IV, yes, but he wasn't that sick, or that weak. It was crazy that none of the doctors found it suspicious. They probably just didn't want all the bother. A stage IV dies, why have any additional paperwork?

My mother wasn't going to have a good death. I'd see to that.

## THIS NOTEBOOK IS THE PROPERTY OF ALFRED KALATCHIK

*For use only by its intended recipient, my beloved Marlene Kalatchik. Burn fully to ash after reading.*

*The worst part about intractable, lifelong depression is the hope.*

*You think, "This time it'll work. This new medication, or this new therapist, or this shock they're going to deliver to my brain to cause mini-seizures— that'll do the trick." I'll start to have energy again; I'll feel fully alive; I won't be a disappointment to my wife and kids anymore; I won't stay at work until nine at night just because I can't face them; I won't feel like a fraud every time I paste on a smile and read them books; I won't have to perform anymore, I'll just plain feel better.*

*But nothing ever works, does it? I remain a fraud. It's not because I don't love my family. It eats me alive, how much I love them. It's why I try so hard to hide my real self, the one that's full of darkness and loathing, the one I thought would be abolished by marrying a wonderful woman. Instead, I just shackled that wonderful woman to an emotional eunuch.*

*Marlene, you're so good to me. You ask so little, and you do so much. You cover for me. You make sure the kids accept what I give them, and they're grateful for it. That's what kills me. I'm barely around, and when I am, I'm asking them to sit on the couch while I read them books. They're too bloody old for that, and yet, it's what I find I can always do; I can always dig deep enough for that. And they take what I can give, and they love me. God help me, I think Thomas even looks up to me.*

*You know, Marlene, that I've wanted to die for practically as long as I've lived. It's because I've got this blackness inside me, this monster they call depression (such a mild word for such a beast!), and I know that all I am is a burden. You shouldn't have to cover for me anymore, and I shouldn't have to fake my way through, and the children shouldn't have to believe in me like I'm Santa Claus. I'm a fictional character. I'm a figment of their imagination, and you stoke that. You tell them about how important I am at work, you build me up in their eyes, so that by the time I get home—this lump who reads to them—they think it's a by-product of my incredible relevance.*

*And I appreciate that, I do, but it torments me, too. I've been living with my own personal torment for forty years now, and I'm ready to stop.*

*It needs to look like an accident, of course, and in order to truly pull that off, I need an accomplice. Everything done alone is too risky; it's too potentially detectable. But with an accomplice to clean up the mess afterward, it would be foolproof. Any one of the scenarios I'm about to lay out would work; of that I'm certain. I've thought through every angle, every contingency. I would never put you at risk, Marlene. But I can't do it alone. If anything went wrong, the children would be saddled with knowing that their father had killed himself. I can't live with that possibility, but I do, very much, want to die.*

*I am of sound mind, as sound as this mind of mine can be, riddled with depression as it is. I have a death wish, but I come by it honestly. I have tried, and tried, and tried. I can't get better. That's the secret no one wants to admit: Some people cannot be improved.*

*It's my time to go, Marlene. Look within your heart, and you'll know it to be true.*

*Please read the following pages, and consider one of the methods I've described. Choose the one you're most comfortable with, and we'll proceed from there. It'll be better for everyone this way, I'm convinced.*

*I am eternally in your debt, my love.*

## *Marlene*

### Right Now

BECAUSE THERE'S ONLY right now, forever.

Trust me, I've got no reason to lie. When you hear people say they've got nothing left to lose, that's the big lie, right there. As long as you're alive, you've got a life to lose. As for me, I'm no longer hamstrung by mortality.

But even the dead have regrets. I've made mistakes. Countless, untold numbers of mistakes. I've hurt my children, damaged them, and how can that not haunt me?

I never knew that ghosts could be haunted.

I'm in a sort of exile—purgatory, perhaps?—and I can't see or hear anything going on. I can't haunt those I've left behind, I can only imagine what's happening in my wake. I have to hope that things played out as I intended, as I did my best to orchestrate.

At times, I'm consumed by thoughts of the past, and memories of all I've done wrong. There's a lot of time, here in my eternal present, since I don't have a body, or anyone to interact with. I'm a floating head, but not even a head. I'm a wisp, with consciousness.

It's not as bad as it sounds. Well, sometimes it's as bad as it sounds—here in my present, reliving my past, imagining other people's futures.

Sometimes I can enjoy the reliving, and the imagining. I've known joy, and can visualize it for my children. Other times, I get stuck in a loop, like a marathon of reruns of all my mistakes.

None were intentional, or at least, none were conscious. I only learned they were mistakes through the outcome, and the aftermath. I thought I was making the best choices as it was all going on, and even now, in hindsight, I don't know what the right choices would have been, what would have guaranteed that I'd have happy, well-adjusted, successful children who actually love one another, and love themselves, and love me. Parenting is trial and error, unfortunately.

In my defense, I did have exceedingly hard choices to make.

If I'm honest, Thomas was the great love of my life. I don't mean that in any perverse sense. I mean that he was the male who made me feel special, and loved. Intellectually, I knew Alfred loved me very much, but so often, it could only be intellectual; he couldn't do much to show me. He didn't do much, period, outside of work, which, I suppose, was a way he showed me. He left me incredibly well-off.

Did I rely on Thomas too much? Maybe. Did he manipulate me? Probably. But did he love me? Absolutely. Of that I have no doubt.

So when he expressed remorse for leaving like he did and said that he wanted to take care of me, I didn't hesitate. I knew my boy. I knew when he was sincere, and when he wasn't. And that was a giant load of shit.

So why did I say yes to him becoming my caregiver? Because I wanted to see how it would play out. Because I wanted him to live in our home again, and have a chance to experience true remorse. I wanted him to watch me die, and regret what he'd done.

I don't mean that cruelly. It's not that I wanted regret to eat at him forever. Really, I was trying to facilitate the opposite. By taking care of me in my final days, by creating the conditions for a come-to-Jesus moment and a genuine reconciliation, he'd be spared a much more terrible regret later. I fully believed that would happen, that our bond was too strong for any other outcome.

Was it a mistake? Possibly. But if you don't make mistakes in life, you're not trying hard enough.

It was a very peculiar night, with Thomas's fauxpenance and Rae and Simon showing up and her claiming that she'd known about Simon's other children and Thomas going on about how Simon was innocent until proven guilty. (Hadn't he just been proven guilty? There were court documents from two different women. One, I could understand, *maybe*, but two?) Rae was so upset about the plan for me to stop treatment, and I was moved, I truly was. She wasn't ready to let me go. But I couldn't help thinking that she was actually more upset by the idea that Thomas would be the one taking care of me, that he'd usurped the role she didn't even want.

Oh, sure, she made me soups. She came over every day. But she didn't enjoy my company, and I didn't enjoy hers. I'd always wanted it to be different, assumed that I'd be closer with my daughter than my son, because I'd have so much to teach her about womanhood. Only it wasn't different. It was precisely the same: We were a million missed connections. Illness doesn't change the essential dynamics of a family (I think a social worker on the oncology unit shared that profundity). What finally changed for me was that I accepted this was the relationship we had.

I was never at my best in her presence. I complained and I kvetched in a way that I never did with Thomas. He wouldn't have put up with it, for one thing, and for another, he would have gotten me to laugh, even at myself. I like to think that Rae wasn't at her best, either, that alone with Simon or with a friend she could be relaxed and talkative. Funny? It was hard to imagine. But happy. I like to imagine that.

So there we all were, sitting at the table and eating delivered Chinese food—I picked at the rice—and Thomas told Rae more about his plan. "We need to stop feeding the cancer," he said. "So no more milk. No meat. A plant-based diet is the way to go. I'm going to make her lots of shakes, with different nutrients and supplements."

He sounded so enthusiastic that I started to doubt what I'd heard earlier. Maybe his remorse was genuine.

He was sorry we'd missed those years, and he wanted to make it up to me. He wanted me to live.

Rae was eating little and saying even less. Simon, on the other hand, had a voracious appetite and was correspondingly gung-ho about Thomas's plan. He asked Thomas a bunch of questions, and said things like, "That's really cool, man. You really know what you're talking about."

Their mutual support and admiration society was so transparent that I could only smile. Thomas had let Simon off the hook, and now Simon was repaying the favor. Rae and I watched the two of them carry the dinner, though our moods were wildly divergent. Rae was glum, while I felt buoyant. Thomas was going to live with me. If he hadn't truly forgiven me yet, he would. He wouldn't be able to resist. I'd have my son back, fully, and if it was only for a short time before I left the earth, that was fine; if his cockamamie supplements actually worked, so much the better.

The next day, Thomas's friend Ben came over to the house with a trunk full of groceries. Powders, and pills, and supplements, oh my!

"It's so good to meet you," Ben said. He had a shy smile and seemed very deferential to Thomas.

"Likewise," I told him. I wanted to say I'd heard so much about him, but it wasn't exactly true. All I'd gathered was that Thomas trusted Ben implicitly, and that Ben was the one minding the store while Thomas looked after me.

I was installed on the fainting couch, which had

become my default home. My strength really was waning by this point. I hoped that whatever was in those bags could help restore it, even temporarily, so that I could be up for a full game of pinochle. I squinted at Ben. My memory had always been excellent, and I felt sure I'd seen him before. "What's your last name again?"

"It's Hwang." Pronounced "Wang." That was a pretty unforgettable name, especially for someone who looked like him—with features that were almost entirely white, with a splash of Asian.

"You grew up around here, right?" I asked him. It was one of the few morsels Thomas had dropped.

"In Medford," Thomas called from the kitchen where he putting away the food. "Small world, huh?"

"We knew some of the same people. We even went to the same chat rooms," Ben said. He laughed. "Seems so retro, huh? Chat rooms. But they were the precursors to social media. People need to gather. If they can't do it in person, they find a way."

I smiled at Ben. I wanted to like him. From reading between the lines, I understood that Ben helped Thomas when Thomas had nothing. Now Thomas had his own company and a beautiful penthouse in Nob Hill. Given that Thomas had zero business experience and had never exhibited much of a work ethic, I had to believe that was largely due to Ben.

As I forced myself to drink a strange but not entirely unpleasant green concoction that Thomas had made in the Vitamix, I got to observe the two of them. Thomas was just so loose, so comfortable, in the light of Ben's obvious admiration. It was quickly apparent that Thomas had never done any research into homeopathic remedies for cancer; Ben had done it all, right down to the shopping. Ben laughed too loud and too hard at Thomas's every joke; Ben's eyes were trained on Thomas with an avidity that I found startling but Thomas obviously felt at home with it. That was the thing: These two men were utterly at home with one another. They were the ones with private jokes, and I was a spectator. I suddenly, viscerally, knew how Rae must have felt all those years, watching me with Thomas.

I'd never intentionally excluded her. But you know how there are just certain people in the world that you truly get, and others where it always feels like work? Well, Thomas was the former, and Rae the latter, and those differences only grew more pronounced after Alfred's death.

I tried to give both of the children emotional support, which was much easier with Thomas than Rae. She was just so unreachable and yet so breakable, like a piece of china that you only take out of the cabinet on special occasions. She'd never been much for physical affection or for talking, and what other language can you speak to a child in, other than verbal and nonverbal? Sonar?

I'd always been able to communicate with Thomas. He was a rascal, of course—mischievous until his father died, and incorrigible after. Twelve is a terrible age to lose a parent. He was flooded with hormones and grief at the same time. He went a little crazy, and I understood. So I bailed him out of some messes. It wasn't his fault. He was very bright, and had poor impulse control, and no father.

But he had me, completely. I doted on him. We played pinochle and talked for hours. He was a good boy with a penchant for drugs and sex. But don't all teenage boys share those?

Rae was an unhappy child, and she became an unhappy teenager. When I tried to invite her into the circle, to do things with her and Thomas, she either said no or glowered silently. Here's how it seemed: She didn't really want me; she just didn't want Thomas to have me. Because when I did try to connect with just her, to have mother-daughter days, she barely spoke, she almost never smiled. It was like she was merely enduring. We'd go home and Thomas would chatter and she'd stay nearby with a hurt look on her face. Then she cloistered in her room. I probably should have tried harder and paid her more individual attention, and God forgive me for saying it, but she was just so boring. I worked so hard for every crumb out of her mouth, and they were all stale.

Yet there I was, what felt like a hundred years later, excluded from Thomas and Ben's private world, without any clear way in, and I became tongue-tied, unsure of myself. I began to feel resentment, to shut down, to withdraw into myself. And all within the span of an hour! A radical clarity overtook me: This was what Thomas and I had done to Rae.

I'd always assumed Rae was just an inaccessible person; it never occurred to me that I'd molded her into one. My understanding of her magnified tenfold in that instant, and my compassion surged. I would need to make amends.

In the meantime, though, I was on the outs, seeing Thomas and Ben interacting like brothers, except that one was clearly bent on incest. Thomas seemed oblivious to Ben's feelings, but I knew he couldn't have been. It was too apparent, and Thomas had always been very aware of everyone's desires and intentions and how to use those to his best interest. That was Thomas's true genius, and it was at work in front of me. Otherwise, how could Ben be holding down the fort every day at Piping Hot (oh, that name) and still be the one toting groceries to my house and seem grateful for the privilege?

Thomas and Ben went into the sunroom, ostensibly to talk business, and the easy camaraderie fell away quickly. I could hear their raised voices but not the words. Actually, it was only Ben's voice I heard, the agitation unmistakable. When Ben left, he said good-bye without looking at me. He was clearly upset, but Thomas gave no outward sign of having been engaged in a confrontation. He always had a high tolerance for conflict.

If I were Thomas, I would have proceeded with extreme caution when it came to Ben, since Ben seemed to have the business in his hand like a snow globe, but cautious wasn't really Thomas's style. Since Thomas didn't seem to want to talk to me about anything to do with Ben or the business, I kept my advice to myself.

For the next week, Thomas was extremely solicitous in a way that reeked of either manipulation or remorse. It was hard for me to decipher. I was feeling weaker, and my bone pain was getting worse. Advil wasn't enough anymore, and the hospice nurses were pushing codeine now.

I thought about resisting, as I had my whole life when it came to medication, but what was the point really?

Even with Thomas around all the time (especially because Thomas was around), I found myself yearning for Rae. It was a comfort to sit in straightforward silence, not to have to question her motives. She was my child, and she wanted me to live. How very refreshing!

Since being the third wheel to Thomas and Ben, I also felt a greater identification than ever before. I wanted to express my sympathy and my sorrow for her, and to apologize for having played such a key role in her torment. But it was so very hard to find the words. How do you begin to express that kind of regret? I wanted to grow closer to her, though I had no idea how to make that happen. Additionally, she'd started bringing Simon with her frequently, like some sort of buffer. Against me, or Thomas, or both?

Maybe she thought that if I spent more time with Simon, I'd begin to like him, or at least grow used to him, like a weed that you start to mistake for grass. Fat chance. Rae had had a hard life, and she deserved better than this man who ran around knocking up women, plural. I hadn't protected her well enough when she was younger, and I intended to find some way to rectify that now.

When Rae was younger, our neighborhood bordered some woods (since eradicated to make room for further development, and local parents were thrilled that their teenagers could no longer party under the tree cover). Rae liked to take walks through those woods by herself.

I never worried. It was daylight, and our neighborhood was a safe one.

One Saturday afternoon in March when she was newly fourteen, Rae took off walking, and an hour later, I received the call every parent dreads. There was a four-lane boulevard on the other side of the woods and Rae had run into traffic and been struck by a car. She was in surgery to repair the internal bleeding in her abdomen.

Thomas was just as panicked as I was. I would have expected concern, but this was utter terror. We rushed to the hospital, where the wait seemed interminable to us both. When we were finally able to see Rae in the recovery room, Thomas and I clutched each other in relief. He came through the door with me and Rae began screaming: "He did this, he did this, get him out of here!" I couldn't recall when, if ever, I'd heard her raise her voice.

I didn't know what to do. I wound up hustling Thomas out because obviously, Rae was in no condition to handle that type of upset. She wasn't in her right mind, and it was no time to challenge her fallacies. "I'm just so glad you're alive," I told her. "The surgery was a success, but it's important to stay calm."

She didn't want to stay calm. She wanted to talk to me and to the police. I'd never seen her in such a voluble state. I'd heard head traumas could cause personality changes, but the doctors said that her injuries were concentrated in her abdomen and pelvis, and had been repaired fully. There would be no lasting injuries, no permanent damage. Rae was a tremendously lucky girl.

"I didn't just run out into traffic," Rae said. "I was chased."

She said that she'd been on the main trail so she was relatively easy to find. It was unmarked but she knew the path well, as did anyone who lived as close as we did. And by anyone, she meant Thomas.

She heard rapidly approaching footsteps behind her and when she glanced back, she knew, instantly, that the figure in the ski mask, wielding a large knife—a cleaver, to be more precise—was Thomas.

"It wasn't Thomas," I told her. "He was with me."

Rae gave me a look so scathing, so seething with hatred, that I once again had to doubt the doctors' conclusion that there had been no head injury. This wasn't my daughter. "You're lying for him."

There was nothing I could say. It was the truth.

The police thought Rae's version of events was preposterous. I tried to fight for her, insisting that there had to have been a man, a stranger, who had been similar in appearance to Thomas. I told them about the peeping Tom a few months before, but they didn't believe me. They thought I was just trying to help Rae save face. "A guy was looking in your daughter's window, and you never called the police?" I was so embarrassed. Why hadn't I done more? I'd been derelict of duty, but I wasn't lying. Yet the police wouldn't hear it.

They pointed out that it had been broad daylight and none of the other drivers had seen anyone in a ski mask wielding a knife. If they had, there would obviously have been 911 calls, in a neighborhood like ours. The police had found no supporting evidence in the woods, either. So with no witnesses or forensics to back up her story, it seemed to them to be just that: a story. "I'd keep her away from horror movies," one of the officers told me with a nasty smile. I wanted to smack the grin off his face.

One of the things that made the officers most suspicious was that Rae kept insisting it wasn't a stranger, that it had to be her brother. "I know what I saw," she said over and over. But Thomas had been with me during that time period. We'd been playing pinochle.

Under the strain of police questioning, I admitted that yes, Rae wasn't the most stable. She had been in therapy for years; she was bullied at school; she was a deeply unhappy girl with a lot of resentment toward her brother (whatever the sibling version of an Oedipal complex was, she had it). The more I talked, the more convinced I became of the police's theory—that it had all been a figment of Rae's imagination. Yes, there had been a peeping Tom, but would a boy with a crush chase Rae into traffic while wearing a ski mask and brandishing a knife? It was absurd. It was, in a word, delusional.

Now I saw that was the most convenient belief for me to adopt, since it let me off the hook for not calling the police about the peeping Tom. Rae had never known about the boy. I hadn't wanted to frighten her unnecessarily, when she was already so prone to frights. I felt that I'd taken care of the problem by locking the shed and upgrading the locks on our windows and doors. When I'd confronted the boy that night, he'd been more scared than I was. I was confident that we'd never hear from him again.

After she was discharged from the hospital a week later, she started an intensive outpatient psychiatric program. That meant that she spent five days a week, six hours a day, in a psych ward.

I never told Thomas about her accusations, and I think Rae was afraid to tell him. She was afraid to go home and live with him. No matter how much I tried to reassure her, even when I described just how upset he'd been to learn she was in the hospital, she insisted that she knew the truth.

"He did it, Mom," she wept. "I know he did. Stop protecting him."

"I'm not protecting him," I said.

"The day before," she said, "I told him that I was going to expose him. I was going to tell you about all the things he was doing."

"So tell me now."

What Rae told me was nothing new, just the usual. Sex and drugs and skipping school and a little bit of larceny. When money went missing, I always knew it was Thomas. It was never large sums.

Rae didn't really have anything on her brother, and Thomas would have known that. He wouldn't have had a motive, and he didn't have the opportunity. I knew he wouldn't have had the stomach for it, either. Thomas got in fistfights occasionally, but nothing like this.

I didn't think Rae was crying wolf or framing her brother, though the police thought that those were real possibilities. "We see a lot of manipulation in girls this age," one said—the same one who made that crack about horror movies. What could I do? Knowing that Thomas had been with me the whole time, and that there'd been no evidence of a pursuit through the woods, I had two options. I could see Rae as sick, or as a manipulative liar. I chose the former.

I told Rae, "I believe that you believe it." After that, Rae clammed up. For years, actually, and she hadn't been a real chatterbox to begin with. She never said it directly, but I see now that she felt betrayed by me, and when I think of it from her perspective, I get it: Instead of Thomas being punished, she was the one labeled as crazy.

She believed that I was lying for Thomas, that I'd invented an alibi for him. What I believed was this: that something had happened to Rae, but that it had happened in her own mind. The internal can be as real as the external, and just as destructive.

Maybe it was because I'd been thinking about the accident, and about the peeping Tom. Maybe that's why everything slipped into place in the most awful way when Ben came to my house for the second time, and I knew where I'd seen Ben before.

He was bearing still more bags (why couldn't Thomas at least buy his own groceries?), and I noticed something strange: He had an identical build to Thomas, and they not only dressed alike in their jeans and T-shirts, but they shared the same low-center-of-gravity walk. Ben was patterning himself on Thomas, which was creepy enough, but that wasn't what made my blood run cold.

With a ski mask on, Ben could have been Thomas's doppelganger.

From there, it just seemed so obvious. The chat room. Living one town over. So Thomas had known Ben all those years ago. When Ben was peeping on Rae, it was deviant all right, but not in the way I'd assumed. Rae hadn't had an admirer; she'd had an enemy.

Was Thomas really behind Rae's "accident" after all? Had he put Ben up to it?

I didn't want to believe that. Yet it was hard to imagine that nebbishy Ben had taken it upon himself to dress up in a ski mask and chase Thomas's sister into traffic.

But Ben looked like Thomas. Why would Thomas frame himself?

I remembered how upset Thomas had been when he found out Rae was in the hospital. Was that because the prank had gone wrong and Rae wasn't supposed to get hurt, or because she *was* supposed to get hurt but he was suddenly sick with guilt? Or was it possible Thomas had nothing to do with it at all?

I couldn't fathom what Ben's motive would be, without Thomas's involvement, and yet I couldn't come up with any sort of motive for Thomas at all.

My head was throbbing. I couldn't begin to contend with these questions. My pain had been spreading along with the sites of the cancer, and I'd been getting headaches as well as bone pain. But this was something different. I felt like my skull was trying to expand outward to twice its size, like it couldn't contain the information my brain was trying to absorb.

If Thomas had really been guilty all these years, then

Rae had been telling the truth, and I'd treated her like she was crazy.

And here he was, feeding me protein shakes and God only knew what else. Was I being watched over by an attempted murderer, and his accomplice?

I groped for the codeine pills on the TV tray next to the couch and gulped them down dry. I didn't want to ask Thomas to bring me some water. Who knew what he'd put in the water?

Ben made another grocery delivery, and something was obviously wrong between him and Thomas that day. There was no lighthearted banter. Or rather, Ben was brooding, and Thomas was ignoring it, acting like his usual self. Steam would soon be coming out of Ben's ears. I could see that whatever was going on between them was reaching a boiling point, yet Thomas wasn't dignifying it, and maybe that was part of what was angering Ben. His feelings seemed entirely irrelevant to Thomas, and even if the root was business, isn't money the number one thing that couples fight about, what ultimately leads to divorce? Money is about the balance of power, and maybe Ben was tired of theirs.

When I'd confronted Ben all those years ago outside Rae's window, I'd been wrong in my assessment. He truly was dangerous. And so was Thomas.

I had nearly gotten my little girl killed because I'd been so determined to believe the best about Thomas. I couldn't make that mistake anymore.

I wouldn't eat or drink anything that came from Ben's

grocery bags. I told Thomas that I had very little appetite, which was true, and that all I wanted was to eat processed foods. As in, things right out of packages like Hostess cupcakes, or right out of cans and bottles, like soda or sparkling water. Thomas chastised me for eating so many simple carbs; he said that wasn't the anti-cancer diet at all. I told him that I was sorry to disappoint him, I just couldn't do the diet. His disappointment seemed genuine but I didn't know how interpret that. Was he disappointed that he wasn't nursing me back to health, or disappointed that he couldn't poison me into an even earlier grave?

As much as I'd resisted medication my whole life, I also hadn't experienced this kind of escalation of physical pain. There was talk about oxycodone, but I was afraid. I needed to keep my wits about me. I worried about "accidental" overdose at Thomas's hands, so I kept all my pill bottles under my blanket to reduce the possibility of tampering. Those were not comfortable days, I'll tell you that. It was not shaping up to be a good death.

I was more tired all the time, and it took greater energy to speak, but my eyes still worked fine. I could watch. And what I observed were whispered, fevered conversations between Thomas and Ben, and furtive glances between Rae and Simon. They were each in their own little clubs, and I was the odd woman out. It made me, honestly, more ready to go. I didn't feel like I had much to cling to anymore. But before I went, I would find out the truth about Thomas. I had to know if I'd turned a blind eye to a monster. And if he was a monster, I had to take care of him. I owed that to Rae.

"You really should eat, Mom," Thomas told me. I was on the fainting couch, as always. How I had grown to despise that couch, but there was no time for one last remodel. "How else are you going to get your strength back?"

"Maybe I'm not."

"I have some stuff I need to take care of today. Ben's going to come out and stay with you, okay?"

Was Ben coming to do Thomas's dirty work? To finish me off? "No, it's not okay."

"What do you mean?" He was still standing, and he had his jacket on. That meant Ben would be here imminently.

"This is my house, and I decide who comes and who goes." I stared him down. I needed to look formidable, at least. "What's going on, Thomas? Why are you really here?"

"To take care of you. We've gone over this." He said it patiently, like he was dealing with a child. Or a crazy person. Maybe I was going crazy. I was certainly paranoid.

"What do you really want from me? Just go on and ask. I can't stand the suspense any longer."

The only thing I could think of was, he'd come back to avenge his father. But real life wasn't some Shakespearean tragedy. Killing me wouldn't bring back his father.

Besides, he had it all wrong. Alfred had wanted me to kill him for years before I was willing to do it. He gave me that awful notebook well before his cancer diagnosis.

Alfred was a good man, but a disturbed one. I didn't find that out until after our wedding—no, it was later than that. It was after I'd gotten pregnant with Thomas.

I'd always thought Alfred was reserved, courtly, a true gentleman; I never suspected depression. He apologized profusely over the years, and urged me to leave him. But the pregnancy had happened quickly, and with kids involved, I didn't want to be on my own, disgraced. What would my family have said? It would have confirmed that I was just as worthless as they'd always thought, not even able to marry well, or to persevere. They had plenty of money, but love? None to spare.

I believe Alfred's chain-smoking was a slow suicide attempt. When he was diagnosed with lung cancer, he was actually happy. He'd finally find relief. He convinced me to do what I wouldn't have under other circumstances. The irony was how convoluted many of the plans in his notebook were, and how simple it wound up being. I helped him overdose on his prescribed medication, and no one asked any questions. Assisted suicide wasn't legal, but I'm sure it happened all the time, and people turned a blind eye.

Thomas and Rae never suspected, same as neither of them seemed to suspect that their father wasn't merely a taciturn workaholic but profoundly depressed. It's amazing, what we can overlook.

I thought that Thomas had put the pieces together over the years, smart as he is, and then one day, a newsmagazine was doing a piece on assisted suicide. I mentioned something about Alfred, as casually as if Thomas already knew. Boy, had I been wrong.

I watched it dawn on him; I watched him rewrite his family history; I watched him begin to hate me.

He left in the night, with only a bag full of clothes. He didn't take the car I'd bought him, or the cell phone. I had no way to reach him, and no leads on where he'd gone. He was a grown man so I didn't have his friends' last names or phone numbers. There was no one to call.

If I'd been able to reach him, I'm not sure what I would have told him, how far I would have been willing to go. Would I have shown him Alfred's suicide book? I'd made the decision years before not to sully his and Rae's opinion of their father by divulging the depression. But suddenly, that information was currency. If Thomas had known that his father had wanted to die for years, that I had made sure he had Alfred as long as he did, and I had only succumbed to Alfred's wishes when he would have been taken from us within a year anyway, that might have made the difference. But it would have been a last resort.

I had my chance now. The notebook was in the safe, with my will and other important papers. Should I take it?

Thomas's memory of his father meant so much to him. I didn't want to destroy it, not unless I absolutely had to.

If Thomas had really been involved in Rae's accident—no, it wasn't an accident at all, I had to stop calling it that—then he would deserve the most severe punishment. But it hadn't come to that yet. There was still a chance my boy was innocent.

"What do you really want from me?" I asked Thomas again.

He remained silent for a long minute. He was actually considering telling the truth. Then the doorbell rang.

"I want you to feel better, Mom," he said quietly, and he went to let Ben in.

As much as I disliked the idea of being alone with Ben, as helpless as I knew I was, I thought that both Ben and Thomas were too stupid to do anything as obvious as putting a pillow over my face. If they were going to take me out, they'd cover their tracks better than that. I was going to die, but my gut said that it wouldn't be today, and this was my golden opportunity. I didn't think Ben was nearly as smooth as Thomas. No one could lie like my son.

Thomas ushered Ben into the living room. "Ben's going to stay with you, okay?" he said, walking toward the door. Over his shoulder, he called out, "Love you, Mom!"

Ben made a big show of greeting me, but once the front door had slammed shut behind Thomas, Ben pulled out his phone. He sprawled in the large upholstered chair opposite me, scrolling and texting. I might as well not even have been there. He didn't even ask if I needed anything.

I felt what I'd felt all those years ago, when I found him on that ladder: This little twerp was no match for me.

"I know who you are," I said. I didn't even feel afraid. After all, what did I really have to lose? My days were just about numbered.

He looked up.

"You knew Thomas in high school. You knew Rae, too, didn't you? I caught you climbing up a ladder on the side of our house."

"You're confusing me with someone else." He was not half the liar Thomas was. Not even an eighth.

"I thought you were interested in Rae, but it was Thomas, wasn't it? Or were you interested in Rae, too? I know young people can swing all different ways. Bisexual, pansexual, trisexual. You do it all, don't you?" I smiled at him, like we were having a friendly chat.

"Thomas told me you get confused, since your illness. That there are spots on your brain, and they give you headaches. Is your head hurting? Can I get you medication or anything?"

He was the one trying to confuse me. Playing mind games with the dying? Tsk-tsk, Ben. It was on now. I'd just had a nap, and I was the feistiest stage IV he'd ever meet. "Where did Thomas go?" I asked.

"To take care of some business." It was the very same wording Thomas had used.

"Don't you take care of all his business?"

"He's the CEO. Some responsibilities are his alone." He returned to his phone.

"Even as a teenager, you were taking care of his business, weren't you? You chased Rae that day."

His eyes stilled on the phone but he didn't look up. He was afraid to, same as he'd been that night I found him on the ladder. I thought at the time that it was because he was ashamed of what he'd done, but now I realized he just feared the consequences of his actions. "Again," he said, "you're confusing me with someone else."

"You probably just wanted to scare her. You were trying to help Thomas deal with his problem sister. You didn't know she'd run into the street like that. Or did you?"

I could see his whole body had frozen up.

"Did you want her to run into the street, Ben?"

"I don't know what you're talking about."

"Did you want her to get hurt, or didn't you? Did Thomas?"

I could see he was practically quaking, just as he'd had trouble climbing down the ladder on his trembling legs all those years ago, and that only emboldened me. I decided to press my advantage. It was time to find out what Thomas really knew, since that was all that really mattered. This was the most alive I'd felt in I didn't know how long.

"You know," I said, conspiratorially, "he's never going to love you. Not the way you love him. It doesn't matter what you do for him, or what you risk. That was true then, and it's true now."

Ben didn't answer, but the tendons in his neck tightened visibly. He was listening.

"Rae didn't really have anything on Thomas. She couldn't expose him, because I knew everything. And Thomas knew that." I was advancing the theory I liked best: that Thomas had no motive, that somehow Ben had taken all this upon himself, that my son was innocent. "When you chased Rae, you weren't really helping him. You weren't doing anything at all, except hurting an innocent young girl."

He looked physically incapable of speech. He looked sick.

"I'm not going to tell the police. There was no proof then so there won't be any proof now. You covered your tracks amazingly well, for someone so young." I feigned admiration. "How did you do that? Did you read a lot of police procedurals, watch a lot of crime movies? Or were you just a prodigy in that as well as computers?" Or he'd just watched too many horror movies, like the detective said. A cleaver and a ski mask? It would have been laughable, if it hadn't nearly killed Rae. My poor girl.

"You've got it all wrong." It came out in a whisper.

"So you didn't try to kill Rae?"

"Of course not." I practically had to read his lips.

"You meant to scare her, to tell her not to mess with Thomas. That's why you were dressed like him. Though he'd never wear a ski mask, not even when he's skiing. He doesn't like to cover that pretty face. It's his moneymaker." It was humor, yes, but it was true. I wanted Ben comfortable. I wanted a full confession, because I wasn't sure I could entirely trust my read on the situation. After all, what I still wanted was for Thomas to be innocent, and my instincts had always pointed me in that direction. I was also growing more tired by the second. This had to go quickly. "You didn't mean for her to get hurt, did you?"

"Of course not," he said again, and I saw that he really wanted me to know that. Then he added quickly, "Because I wasn't there. I had nothing to do with whatever happened to Rae."

I pretended I hadn't heard his addendum. "And Thomas thought he was meeting you for the first time at that self-help meeting." Please, let it be so. Thomas was a manipulator, an opportunist, but he wasn't evil. From Ben's pause, I understood. "Thomas didn't remember you, but you remembered him. You followed him around when he was a teenager. You meant to look into Thomas's room that night, didn't you? You wanted to watch him sleep."

"It wasn't like that. I wasn't some stalker."

"How was it?"

"We hooked up sometimes. He was just too fucked up to remember, and he didn't want to think of himself that way."

"Think of himself how?"

"As gay. Not that I'm gay."

Oh, right. The fluid sexuality of his generation—he's not gay, he's just gay for Thomas. "So you weren't memorable enough for Thomas, and he didn't want to be seen with you in daylight?"

"I didn't approach him in daylight. It would only happen at parties."

"Were you in love with him?"

Ben went silent.

"What I don't understand," I said, "is your endgame. You didn't approach Thomas in daylight because he was only interested in you while he was 'fucked up' at parties, so instead you connected with him in some chat room, and then you decided somehow it would help your cause to chase his sister into traffic?"

"I was a teenager." He looked at me as if appealing for sympathy. "I didn't know what I was doing. I realize now that it doesn't make any sense at all, and if I could, I'd take it all back. I'd undo what happened." I was watching him impassively. Forgiveness would not be forthcoming.

"I guess I thought somehow if I scared Rae, she wouldn't tell on him, and his life would be easier, and he'd be grateful . . . But she didn't have anything to tell, and she wasn't supposed to get hurt. Once she did, I could never let him know it was me."

"You were a lovesick teenager then, I get it. But what's your endgame now, Ben?" I left the rest unsaid: You're going to help Thomas kill his dying mother and then he'll love you? You're going to run his company for him and then he'll love you?

I could feel bad for this idiot in front of me except that Rae nearly died, and she'd been tortured for years, thinking her brother was the culprit and her mother was colluding with him.

"Are you going to tell Thomas or should I?" I asked.

"He wouldn't believe you," Ben finally said. "We're too tight."

"Thomas uses people. He turned his back on his own mother, so what makes you think you're so special?" I was getting to him, that was apparent, but my voice was taking on a drowsy quality. I was fading fast. There wasn't much more to say, really, but I wanted to inflict maximum damage. For Rae. It was too little, too late, I knew that, but I'd take my stab. "He can just hire someone to do what you do. Silicon Valley is a half hour away."

Scorn and rage battled for dominance on Ben's face. "No one would do what I do."

"That's just it, Ben. You need to have some boundaries, some pride. There have to be lines you won't cross. He knows you'd do anything for him, and that's why he'll never, ever be with you. Not in the way you want. Because he doesn't respect you.

"Or maybe," I said, and now I was the one almost whispering, I was just so bloody tired, "you like it this way. It must be an exquisite form of torture, very *Fifty Shades of Grey*, and Thomas doesn't even know he's playing." Or he does, all too well. "Stop doing his dirty work, starting now."

"You've got it all wrong," he said again, his voice choked. It sure didn't look like much fun, this arrangement he was locked into with Thomas. But he deserved far worse after what he'd done.

I forced my eyes to stay open, fixed on his. "Don't ever come back to my house again. And while you're at it, get the hell out of my son's life."

For a boy wonder, he wasn't thinking so fast on his feet. He sat there, mute, outfoxed by a woman who was close to dead.

"I can't leave you alone," he finally managed. "Thomas said—"

"Go now," I clarified.

And he did.

The confrontation with Ben exhausted me beyond measure. When I next opened my eyes, it was dark. I could hear voices being raised and lowered in the kitchen. I followed the sounds, groping and gripping my way along the wall like an invalid, and then I slid downward when I was close enough to hear more distinctly.

"You need to tell her to start treatment again," Rae was saying. "You're the only one she'll listen to."

Oh, Rae. Didn't she see? I was too weak for more chemo. I ached for my sweet, naïve girl, the one I'd so stupidly spurned all these years, the one fighting for my life. I'd chosen Thomas over her. I'd bet on the wrong horse, and I was paying the price now, but Rae had been paying for years.

"She doesn't want more treatment," Thomas answered. "This is about respecting her wishes."

"Bullshit," Rae said. You tell him! "You're working an angle. I don't know what it is, but I'm not scared of you anymore."

"Why would you ever have been scared of me?"

"You know why."

"I really don't."

"You want me to say it right to your face?" A pause. "Fine. I will. You chased me through the woods, into oncoming traffic. You tried to kill me. I let Mom call it an accident, but you know what it really was, and I know what it really was, and Simon's got my back. He's not going to let anything happen to me."

I pictured Thomas's face, too shocked to respond. Was he shocked because he really had no idea she felt that way, or shocked that she found the courage to come right at him?

That's the moment when I knew I had truly hardened my heart to my own child. Because I didn't care about his answer.

All I cared about was Rae. I was so proud of her. After all these years, she'd finally found her voice.

"That's what you think?" Thomas sputtered.

"It's what I know."

"Someone chased you through the woods and you thought it was me?"

"I know it was you." She sounded triumphant. She had him on the ropes.

"You were different after the acc— after that happened. You wouldn't even look at me. I just never got it. I didn't understand." Another pause. "She should have told me."

"What?" Rae was less certain now.

"Mom. She should have told me what you thought. Why didn't she tell me? Then you and I could have talked. I could have tried to fix things."

He was blaming me? Blame Ben. Blame yourself, Thomas. If Thomas hadn't led Ben on all those years ago, Ben would never have gone after Rae. Thomas had used people his whole life and gotten away with it. It came to me that he was the only one of us who hadn't yet paid. He made millions without seeming to lift a finger because of his henchman Ben. He never got his hands dirty.

"I didn't want Mom to tell you." But Rae was starting to sound like her old equivocating self.

"You were fourteen. What the hell did you know?"

"I knew I'd been attacked. And I knew who did it." There was doubt in her voice now.

"All these years, we could have fixed things. We could have talked. Like we are right now. Like two adults. But she didn't want that. She wanted to keep you down, don't you get it? She wanted you to need her.

Was he right? My conscious intent was to keep things from getting even worse, for everyone, but somewhere inside, had I been trying to prevent them from reconciling? All along, had my truest motive been to keep them apart, keep Thomas all for myself, keep Rae down?

No, none of that was true. Thomas was sabotaging me. He was taking away my one good child. Perhaps that had been his intention all along in coming back: to make sure that I died all alone as a way to punish me for killing his father.

"Just tell her I stopped by, okay?" I could hear Rae's disorientation. He was getting to her, and she didn't want to be forced to revise her history. She had reached a conclusion that worked for her; she'd screwed up her courage, found her voice, and now, she was left wondering.

"No," he told her, and even I could make out the urgency, the sincerity. "Stay."

"Let go of my arm."

"Sorry. I just . . . I want us to talk more. Let's get out of here. Let's go somewhere."

"And leave her by herself? She's dying, Thomas. See, it's always about you."

"This is about us. She's going to die, Rae, and we're still going to be here. Let's not fuck up our chance, okay?"

"She's going to die because you're making her whey protein with spirulina—which she doesn't drink anyway—when she should be doing more chemo."

She was crying. Oh, Rae. She still didn't want to let me go, after everything, after I'd been so awful to her.

Somehow, I found my way to my feet, and into the kitchen. I clutched for Rae, and she grabbed me, holding me up. "Let's get you to bed," she told me.

"I'm proud of you," I said. "Telling him your truth."

"Mom! What the fuck!" It was an anguished yelp. "You know I was with you!"

I paid him no mind. "I'm so tired," I murmured. "Thank you, Rae. Thank you, sweetheart."

She helped me to my bedroom. I knew that what would help Rae the most was to be believed, once and for all. No qualifications, no alibis. After all, Thomas had been behind it all. She wouldn't have been hit by that car without him.

Rae tucked me in carefully. She'd make an excellent mother someday. I was sorry that I wouldn't be around to see it. I looked deeply in her eyes and told her, "I believe you."

Thomas left my house that night, never to return. Or so he thought.

It was time. I would die within a few days, a week, at most.

I'd been arranging my own death for a while, in my mind. I always knew I wouldn't just let cancer win, the same as with Alfred. It was always a question of which person would do the honors, what would be the most advantageous end.

For a while, I'd thought that it would be Thomas administering the overdose. That would be poetic justice, the closing of the circle. He tore out of the house after learning that I'd done it for his father, too full of judgment to allow me any explanation. It seemed fitting that he should be forced to live with his own hypocrisy. But he'd slipped out of my grasp again, and this time, I was ready to let him go.

I learned from my Twitter feed that Thomas had been served legal papers by Ben. The company basically wasn't his anymore; now it was Ben's.

I'm sure Thomas hadn't seen that coup d'état coming. He'd believed in his absolute power over Ben, had assumed that Ben's love would be bigger than greed. Ben had most likely been marshalling his forces for a while, gearing up for a takeover, waiting for his moment. Maybe that moment would never have come if it hadn't been for our little conversation; I'd pushed him over the edge. Or maybe this whole time, Ben had just been getting Thomas out of the way, encouraging Thomas to take care of his dying mother, so that Ben would be able to enact the final phase of his operation. Unrequited love gets tiresome after a while. So does exploitation.

Thomas probably never even knew it was exploitation. Sometimes manipulation just came so naturally to him, and his justifications were so automatic, that he thought of every arrangement as mutually beneficial.

I hadn't meant for Thomas to lose everything. In my ideal scenario, Ben would have quit and Thomas would have learned to clean up his own messes. He'd have to grow up and stop using people. I didn't think his comeuppance would be so severe, but perhaps it was a lifetime's worth in one fell swoop. Thomas had always been so insulated from consequences before, I'd seen to that—just one of my many mistakes.

So he was out of the running for killing me.

I wanted my death to benefit Rae the most. She'd endured so much, I'd wronged her profoundly, and yet she'd remained loyal to the bitter end. She deserved a generous inheritance, though she needed to break free of that Simon.

It had always been obvious that Simon was an operator, and I certainly didn't change my opinion the more Rae brought him around. Quite the contrary—I detested him more when I saw his chameleon tendencies. He was one way with her, another with Thomas, and a third way with me. It was like he thought I was some sort of grande dame, a figure from *Downton Abbey*.

But Rae was determined to marry him, despite him being a deadbeat dad. So how about making him a murderer?

Once Thomas stopped being my full-time caregiver, Rae said that she'd take a leave from work and do it. I told her not to be silly, that hospice was sufficient, but really, what I was thinking was, it won't be long now. So I made sure to text Simon and ask him to come over at a time when Rae wouldn't be here.

He was between jobs so he was extremely available. That was another thing that bothered me: how little it bothered him to simply not work. He would be all over that inheritance if he had the chance.

I made sure that I was propped up on the fainting couch instead of reclining. Recumbence was just too vulnerable. Once Thomas had disappeared (again), I'd felt safe enough to start taking the oxycodone. But not that day. I needed to stay sharp. That meant I was trying not to grimace through the entire conversation.

Simon kissed me on the cheek and then took both my hands in his, the way he'd seen me do with Rae. What a phony. "How are you feeling, Marlene?"

"Go on, sit down." I meant that he should take the other couch or at least the chair, but no, he had to scooch in beside me, invading my personal space. Every fiber of my being protested. This was not a trustworthy man.

"I did what you asked. I didn't tell Rae about this." Suck-up.

"Thank you. This conversation would just be too hard for her. She needs you to be strong." He nodded solemnly. "I'm in pain all the time. I don't feel like I can continue this way. I don't want to."

His brow furrowed. "And Rae . . . ?"

"I don't tell her about the pain. You know how sensitive she is. And I can't tell her that I'm ready to go, or that I need someone's help to do it. Now that Thomas isn't around . . ." He just stared at me. ". . . everything I have is going to Rae. To you and Rae, since you'll be spending your lives together."

"Marlene, I don't feel right having this conversation without Rae here."

"I understand. You share everything, don't you?"

"We try to."

"Then you know that this is tearing Rae up, and that it could drag on for months, with me in pain and your lives on hold."

"We've been talking about moving the wedding up. So you can be there."

No, no, no! "I can't hang on, Simon, much as I wish I could. I want to be set free from the pain, and I want Rae to be set free from the uncertainty, from spending her time waiting for her mother to die. I want her to get on with her life, with you. If you can help me, I'll give you my full blessing."

"What is it you want me to do?"

"Get Seconal. It's easy. You can do it on the Internet. Then administer it and make sure that I'm not suffering. Make sure it goes off okay. And afterward, take care of my daughter."

I could see he was considering. "I don't think I can do that," he said finally. "I don't want to lie to her."

"Do you want to see the will? Rae gets everything. And she's marrying you—as long as you have my blessing." I was pretty sure Rae intended to marry him regardless but I had him thinking. Doubting.

"She wants you to be there. Why don't I see if we can get a wedding together ASAP?"

He wanted to make sure he and Rae were married before he would kill me. Some people are so selfish.

"The longer you wait," I said, "the greater the chance that Thomas and I will reconcile. He lost his business, did you know that?"

So it was decided.

I said my good-byes without anyone knowing that's what I was doing, and I have to admit, it was hard not to tell Rae. It was hard to accept that I wouldn't be around to protect her any longer. But she's not quite a damsel in distress anymore. She found her strength when it came to Thomas, and I have to believe she'll continue to possess it after Simon's gone.

I left a note among my effects—how strange, to have effects—that I knew Rae would find. Across the envelope it said, "Open in the event of my death," and it talked about Simon's rapacious behavior, his untoward interest in my will, and my fear that he wouldn't be able to wait for cancer to claim me. I said that I'd seen a suspicious package from a pharmacy in Nottingham, England; he'd gotten a strange look on his face and claimed he was having trouble sleeping.

Rae will be okay, Rae *is* okay. I tell myself that all the time. Because what no one tells you about death is that it's like a big screening room. All you can do is replay your life. You don't get to look down on your loved ones and see what they're doing; you just have to hope that they're carrying on. You have to hope that you set them up to have the best lives possible.

I think I did that.

Rae has her happy ending, of sorts: She'll get millions of dollars, and she'll be free of all of us—of me, her ne'er-do-well brother, and the scoundrel who would have eventually broken her heart anyway and stolen all her money.

I left the house to Thomas, in a manner of speaking. I didn't want him to be homeless, so I set it up that he can't sell it but he can live there for the rest of his life.

I burned Alfred's notebook, just as he'd requested. It wouldn't do anyone any good now. But I think it had served its purpose for Alfred. Fantasizing about suicide plans, researching and jotting down ideas and turning them into meticulous blueprints, believing he might have an early exit—it had made him happy, in his way. But I was happy to see it go up in smoke.

All I've ever wanted is to take care of my family, and now I have. It wasn't such a good life, all told, but it was a reasonably good death.

May I rest in peace.

## Rae

### Right Now

SIMON IS A lot of things, but he's no murderer. The week after Mom died, he confessed to me. He'd helped her. He wanted me to be free of her, and to protect the inheritance, yes, but mostly, it was about rescuing me from her clutches, once and for all. He had proof that she'd tried to recruit him: a copy of the will that she kept in a safe.

So cancer really, finally, had taken its toll on her. She never would have left evidence like that before; she would have had him read it in her presence and give it back. If she hadn't been so sick, she would have covered her tracks better. By the time I found that falsely incriminating note, I already knew the truth.

Simon is a lot of things—many of them very loving and very good—and the most important one of all is that he's the father of my unborn child. I was the one who'd been lax about birth control, taking my pill hours late and sometimes forgetting it altogether, yet he'd been thrilled about the news. He's the one who insisted on a prenup so that I'd know he's here for me, and for the baby, that it's not about the money.

It's kind of sad, how my mother looked around and saw so much manipulation and evil in the world. I've learned to see otherwise. I can see beauty and strength, and I want to let go of ugliness and hatred. I can believe. I can forgive.

I believe that Thomas really was with my mother that day, and when she gave him an alibi, she was telling the truth. Improbable as it may seem, someone else chased me that day. Sometimes the most incredible stories are actually true.

I forgive Thomas for how he treated me. I believe his remorse. I might even let him be an uncle.

I forgive my mother for trying to frame Simon. In her warped way, she wanted to protect me. When she finally told me she believed me, I know it was a lie, since Thomas really was with her that day, but I saw her intent. I understood her heart. And that was enough.

I forgive myself for putting up with way too much shit for way too long. You know how they say God doesn't give you more than you can handle? Well, I'm not sure about that, but people don't give you more than you're willing to tolerate. And the less you tolerate, the better you feel about yourself.

It took me twenty-eight years to learn, and now I finally have something to teach, something to give. It's all going to this little one growing inside me.

I took that letter from my mother, and together, Simon and I burned it to ash. With each lick of the flames, each plume and tendril of smoke, I was purified.

**Don't miss the next thrilling suspense novel**

**from best-selling author**

**Holly Brown**

# THIS IS NOT OVER

**Coming January 2017**

**Click here to preorder!**

**Read on for a sneak peek . . .**

## 1

### *Dawn*

Please note: It is April 23, 2014. You'll have your deposit within seven business days, just like it says on Getaway.com. I've put through a refund to your credit card for the full amount, minus $200 to replace the sheets. I couldn't get the stain out despite professional laundering and bleaching, and it was rather large (gray, about the size and shape of a typical house cat, though the house rental didn't allow pets). That's neither here nor there. At any rate, I already told you about this.

Miranda

THAT'S IT, THE entire e-mail. No *Dear Dawn* or *I'm sorry you had to stalk me to get your deposit* or *Sincerely* or *All the best.* Just *Miranda*. And does she really think I don't know today's date?

I haven't felt anger like this in I don't know how long. No, I know how long. Since before Rob. He's the antidote for all my inadequacies. I'm good enough because I have him in my life. Because I'm the woman he loves. I'm *that* woman now.

Stop reading. Stop rereading.

But I can't.

I'm sitting at my battle-scarred kitchen table, staring at the screen of my five-year-old laptop in my one-bedroom apartment in a rapidly gentrifying neighborhood in Oakland (soon we'll be priced out), and I've been struck dumb. A stain the size and shape of a house cat? Like my husband and I are, collectively, Pigpen from *Peanuts*, and we leave a cloud of ash in our wake?

I'm an honorable (enough) person, and for sure Rob is. If we'd ruined Miranda's sheets, we would've owned up to it. I would've contacted her myself, apologized profusely, and said, "Take my deposit, please." No, I would have bleached the sheets, and if that hadn't worked, I would have run out to the nearest Target in a state of abject mortification and bought a new set (because those were not $200 sheets, I promise you that). Then one or the other of us, Rob or myself—whoever had left the ejaculate or the powder or whatever state (solid, liquid, or gas)—would have sought medical attention immediately, because WTF?

But that sequence of events never took place, because there's no way the stain is real. This woman, this Miranda, is trying to scam us out of our $200, half the amount of the security deposit. She's stealing from me, from us.

*That's neither here nor there.*

She's a thief and a liar, and she's trying to make me feel like I'm filthy, literally. Like I'm beneath her. Sure, she owns an ocean-view house in Santa Monica, and I own nothing, but that doesn't give her the right to . . .

Breathe, Dawn. WWRD—What Would Rob Do?

He'd let it go, because life is too short for grudges. But then, he's never been wronged, not in any way that matters.

*I already told you about this.*

Another lie.

What gets me is that she's so undeserving of that gorgeous house she doesn't even need to live in. It's an extra, a spare. I wonder about the opulence of her first home, if that's her second. How does a person like her get a setup like that? Where's the justice in this world? I bet she doesn't even appreciate her good fortune. I would, if it were mine.

I should be studying. This semester's been brutal, and I'm closing in on graduation. My good fortune is in being with Rob, someone who supports me in finally finishing my college degree. It's not every man who insists that his wife devote herself exclusively to her studies. I am incredibly, insanely, painfully lucky.

But I'm so pissed—both about Miranda's actions and about the snotty, deceitful tone she used to justify them—that I can't concentrate. Miranda stole my husband's hard-earned money, and how can I just let that go? Not to mention she's stealing my time and my energy. She's hijacking my emotions. I'm a slave to my outrage.

It's not only about the $200 (which I could most definitely use); it's the principle. She's trying to shame me, to make me think I did something wrong, something dirty, in order to buy herself what? A dinner? A pair of cashmere socks? That's after we paid her usurious price for a rental that was, admittedly, beautiful, but with no add-ons. No sweet surprises. Not like in Monterey, where we discovered a bidet and two free member passes to the aquarium. We went every day just to stare at the jellyfish, getting lost in their hypnotic undulations, imagining what it would be like to go through life with your own attached parachute, knowing you can never crash.

Monterey was my favorite getaway with Rob, because there was something about that house rental that allowed us to inhabit another life completely for those five days. I could envision a future where Rob and I are members of the aquarium ourselves, regular visitors with our kids, a boy and a girl (twins?) who stand agog as thousands of sardines swim in their circles like a silvery carousel.

It might sound shallow, but I'm pretty confident that Rob and I will have attractive children. Rob's handsome, and I've often heard that I'm beautiful, in an old-school, Christie Brinkley way (blue eyes, big toothy smile, no one suspects that I've been dyeing my long blond hair since I was a teenager).

The truth is, I don't feel beautiful, or even pretty, because I'm barely five-foot-one and at thirty years old, I still have the temperamental skin of a teenager: always at least one pimple, usually more, plus the brown dots that are the slowly healing legacy of pimples past. I'm constantly trying out new skincare products—no, not just products, entire systems. I start with great optimism ("I think I see something! I'm smoother and more supple!"), only to have my skin reassert itself with a vengeance. When people look at me admiringly, I feel like I'm putting one over on them.

Hopefully, our kids will inherit Rob's complexion, among other things.

But back to Miranda, the matter at hand. It's probably unfair to compare her Santa Monica rental to the Monterey house. I'll compare it instead to the one in Mendocino, a pleasant median: with a hot tub perched on a sea bluff, the kitchen sans the Vitamix that was shown in one of the pictures (but not promised in the text so I couldn't officially complain), the mattress that sagged slightly in the center, and the dun-colored days despite being outside the parameters of fog season.

Miranda's house still loses. Six hundred dollars a night and we had to go searching through cabinets to find replacement lightbulbs. Not to mention how loud the dishwasher was, and the hairline crack in the living room ceiling, and the absence of mini-shampoos or bodywashes. I felt her stinginess at every turn. A quarter inch of olive oil left in the bottle, grocery store brand. No spice rack, only salt, pepper, and thyme. How did thyme make the cut? How about some basil, or oregano? Red pepper flakes, for shit's sake?

When Rob and I get away, I'm after five-star accommodations, but in a house rather than a hotel so I can marinate in that lifestyle for a little while. It's the adult version of playing dress-up. I dislike when hosts meet us at the house because then I'm reminded it's theirs, and I have a visual to go with that knowledge. But that's only happened once. Normally, rich people do it like Miranda does, with minimal contact: key in a lockbox, call in an emergency.

Burned-out lightbulbs, lack of basic cooking supplies, and cracks in plaster remind me of my real everyday, where things need replacing and fixing and sometimes you run out. Vacations are for abundance. While Rob and I are away, money is never an object, and that's the biggest break from real life. I even have a different wardrobe for vacation (slinky cocktail dresses for which I scour consignment shops, and stiletto heels instead of wedges), and I start using Crest Whitestrips a month out so I can wear the red lipstick that's too much for everyday.

I'm reborn in those houses. They scrub me clean of all the debris from my past. I'm Dawn 2.0. Because the true American dream is that you don't have to be who you were, you're not where you grew up, you're not defined by the family you left behind or the family that left you behind way before that.

Getaway.com has never let me down before. I read through all the reviews thoroughly before I book. I pay special attention to the three-star ones, which seems to be as low as anyone will ever go, and that's probably because a one- or two-star makes you look like a disgruntled ex-lover, bent on vengeance, not to be widely trusted. As I parse each review, I can tell who has a sensibility similar to mine; I can tell who to believe.

Miranda's house had twenty-seven reviews, and nearly all of them were five stars. There was nothing below a four. People loved the ocean views, the proximity to the pier, and the hospitality, oh, the hospitality! You could call Miranda any time, no need too small. She recommended the most fabulous Thai food; she knew the best car service. When a toilet broke down on Christmas Day, she had a plumber out there within the hour, and she sent flowers afterward, with her apologies.

Who was *that* Miranda? I would have liked to meet her.

*About the Author*

**HOLLY BROWN** is a practicing marriage and family therapist, and the author of *Don't Try To Find Me* and *A Necessary End*. Her blog, "Bonding Time," is featured on Psychcentral.com. She lives with her husband and daughter in the San Francisco Bay Area.

Discover great authors, exclusive offers, and more at hc.com.